Scary! 2

Scary! 2

More stories that will make you scream!

EDITED BY PETER HAINING

BARNES
&NOBLE
BOOKS
NEW YORK

2003 Barnes & Noble Books

ISBN 0-7607-3762-2

Printed and bound in the United States of America

03 04 05 06 07 08 MC 9 8 7 6 5 4 3 2 1

FG

*Let me remind you what the wary fox
once said to the lion: 'Those footprints
directed your way scare me because none
are coming back.'*

The Roman Poet, Horace.
The Odes (65–8 BC)

CONTENTS

RETURN OF THE SCAREMONGERS

An Introduction

What's the *scariest* thing that has ever happened to you?

I remember mine very well – and sometimes, late at night, when I wake up thinking about it – it scares me all over again.

It took place many years ago when I was a young reporter on a local newspaper in rural Essex – a district which then had quite a few isolated little villages scattered with old houses and crumbling buildings.

One Christmas, the editor of my newspaper thought it would be fun to run a story about a local haunted house. There were supposed to be several in the area covered by our paper and, as the newest member of the staff, he volunteered me for the assignment. I was to spend a night in one of these places – my choice (Thanks, a million, boss!) – and then write a feature story about my experiences.

He hoped I'd come face to face with a ghost. *I* wasn't so sure. The spoilsport wouldn't even send one of the paper's photographers to keep me company in case something *did* come to light. He would, though, get someone along the following morning *if* I had anything special to report.

So I selected for my investigation an old, two-storey property which had stood empty and deserted for years on the outskirts of a farming village in north-west Essex. According to local legend, a man had murdered his wife there one night just before Christmas. After he had been arrested, tried and hanged for his crime, the ghost of his wife was said to have returned to haunt the house. Thereafter, a figure with a terrified face would be seen at an upstairs window every year on the anniversary of the awful crime. And, for generations, villagers who knew the story avoided the house like the plague in the days before Christmas.

A few days later when I entered the building for the first time with darkness beginning to fall, the story was still ringing in my head. I'd brought something to eat and a little something else to keep up *my* spirits in case any spirits did materialise. I also had a folding chair and used it to make myself as comfortable as possible in the upstairs room where the murder was supposed to have been committed.

But, as the night went on and nothing happened, I began to think it was, perhaps, just a *story*. To be honest, though, my heart did miss a beat when there was a sudden tapping at the window and, later, when I heard a creaking sound downstairs. (The first turned out to be the branch of a tree knocking on the glass and the other was caused by the wind swinging a broken door on its hinges.)

Just before dawn, though, *something* very scary happened which convinced me never to believe that all ghost stories are rubbish.

I was sitting, half-asleep, in my chair. A glance at my wristwatch had told me that the sun would soon be rising. Then, suddenly, the whole room went terribly cold. One minute the place was chilly, but the next it seemed as if a huge refrigerator door had been opened. There was nothing I could see – but a coldness struck through my clothes as if I were wearing nothing at all.

For what seemed like an eternity – though it was probably no more than a few moments – I sat in my chair unable to breathe. The silence was horribly spooky. The cold air seemed to make time stand still.

In that moment, too, it was if *something* passed right by me in the room.

Almost before this thought had entered my head, a ray of sunshine broke into the room. In that instant, the temperature rose to normal again as if that unearthly refrigerator had been slammed shut.

Had I been in the presence of a ghost? From that moment to this, I have never been sure but I *do* know that it remains the scariest thing that has happened to me.

Which brings me to the stories in this book. Because lots of you enjoyed my earlier anthology, *Scary! Stories That Will Make You SCREAM!* which was first published in 1998, the editor at my publishers (a much nicer chap than that one who sent me out to the haunted house in the dead of night) has asked me to bring together some more of my favourite scary stories.

So I have included several of today's most popular practitioners of fright who did not appear in the first book – including Philip Pullman, Robert Swindells, Dean Koontz, Anne McCaffrey and Alison Prince – as well as some new masters of the genre, like Pete Johnson and Neil Gaiman.

I have also chosen stories by three classic masters of the macabre in order to introduce their work to a new generation of readers. The first is M.R. James who has been called 'the Father of the Modern Ghost Story' and can knock spots off any tale-teller of the supernatural – myself included – as you will discover. Then there is Sir Arthur Conan Doyle who created Sherlock Holmes; here he puts the great detective on the trail of a suspected vampire. Thirdly, Bram Stoker, of whom I need to say no more than that he was the author of *Dracula!* I hope that after you have read their short stories here you will look for others by them, because they were the authors who inspired many of today's great horror story writers.

All of the stories in this collection feature boys and girls in scary situations. Some are brave and resourceful, but most of them – like pretty well all of us – get frightened from time to time. Some of the things that happen to them occur at home, others out in the town or city, a couple even at school and in a club. Just the sort of places we all know, in fact. But in these tales the kids are about to experience things –

just as I did – that none of them expect . . . and will never forget.

So welcome, once again, to the world of the Scaremongers!

Peter Haining,
December, 2001

VIDEO NASTY

Philip Pullman

Martin, Kevin and David are mates. They all go to the same school and like doing the same things. Today they are playing truant – but for a special reason. Martin, who's the oldest and always seems to have plenty of money, has ordered a video from the local newsagents, which the three friends are going to watch in Martin's house while his parents are out. But it's no ordinary video. It's called Snuff Park *and Martin says that someone really gets killed in it. So all three are pretty nervous about what they're going to see. And when a strange boy none of them knows asks if he can come and watch, too, things start to get really scary – especially because the kid seems to know an awful lot about* Snuff Park . . .*

*   *   *

It was a cold grey afternoon in November, and the three boys had been hanging around the shopping precinct since mid-morning. They'd had some chips at midday, and Kevin had nicked a couple of Mars bars from the newsagent's, so they weren't hungry. And until they were thrown out of Woolworth's they weren't cold either; but by half-past three they were cold and fed up, and almost wished they'd gone to school.

'How much longer we got to wait?' said David, the youngest boy, to Martin, the oldest.

Martin was fourteen, thin and dark and sharper than the other two by a long way. He looked at his watch. 'Oh, come on,' he said. 'Let's go and see if it's ready.'

He hunched himself inside his anorak and led the way out of the precinct and down one of the old streets that led towards the canal. The cold wind blew crisp packets and old newspapers around their ankles. The boys turned around two corners and stopped outside a little newsagent's, where one of the windows was filled with a display of video cassettes.

'See if there's anyone in there, Kev,' said Martin.

Kevin opened the door, which jangled loudly. The street was empty, apart from an abandoned Datsun without any wheels that stood in a scatter of broken glass half on and half off the pavement. After a few seconds Kevin came out and said, ' 'S okay.'

The other two went in. The place smelled like all newsagents – a bit chocolatey, a bit smokey, a bit like old comics. There was nothing unusual about it, but David felt his stomach tightening. He pretended to be unconcerned and picked up a paperback that said AQUARIUS: Your Horoscope For 1994. He didn't know if he was Aquarius or what, but he had to look cool.

An old man had come out from the back. He was carrying a mug of tea, and sipped at it before he spoke.

'Yes, lads?' he said.

Martin went up to the counter. 'You got that video in yet?' he said. 'The one you told me about last week?'

The old man took another sip, and narrowed his eyes.

'What one's that? I don't remember you.'

'You said it'd be in today. *Snuff Park*. You told me about it.'

Recognition came into the old man's eyes, and he smiled carefully.

'Course I remember,' he said. 'You got to be careful, that's all. Wait there.'

He put his mug on a shelf and shuffled out. Kevin's frowning, short-sighted eyes flickered to the sweets, but Martin put his hand on his arm, and shook his head. No-one spoke.

After a minute the old man came back with a video cassette, which he put in a brown paper bag. Martin passed over the money; David put back his book and opened the jangling door.

'Bye, lads,' said the old man. 'Enjoy the film.'

'Let's have a look,' said Kevin, once they were outside.

Martin took out the cassette, but there was no picture. There just a plain white label with 'SNUFF PARK. 112 mins' typed in the centre.

'What's mins?' said Kevin.

'Minutes, you berk. That's how long it lasts,' said Martin, putting it back. 'Come on, let's get a cup of tea. I'm perished.'

'Can't we go to your place?'

'Not yet. I told you. They ain't going out till six. We got to hang about till then.'

As they walked past the abandoned Datsun, one of the doors creaked open. David jumped back out of the way. A thin boy of about his age, wearing torn jeans and trainers and a dirty anorak, was sitting in the driver's seat, with his feet on the pavement. He said something quietly and Martin stopped.

'What?' he said.

'What cassette you got?' said the boy. His voice sounded like the sound your feet make in dry leaves.

'What you want to know for?' said Martin.

The boy shrugged. David thought he could smell him: sharp and dirty and somehow cold. Kevin had his hand on the car door.

'*Snuff Park*,' said Martin after a moment. 'You seen it?'

The boy shrugged again, and said 'Yeah'. He wasn't looking at any of them, but down at the pavement. He scuffed the broken glass with one foot.

No-one else spoke, so Martin turned and walked off. The other two followed. David looked back at the boy in the car, but he hadn't moved. Just before they turned the corner, he shut the car door.

In the cafeteria, Martin paid for three cups of tea and brought them to the table by the window where Kevin and David had found a place. David didn't know where Martin got his money from; he assumed Martin's parents gave it to him. He always seemed to have plenty, but he never boasted about stealing it, as Kevin would have done.

He stirred sugar into his tea and watched his reflection in the glass. It was nearly dark outside already.

'What's it about, *Snuff Park*?' said Kevin. 'Sounds crummy.'

'Well it ain't,' said Martin. 'It's a real snuff movie.'

'What's one of them?'

Martin sighed. 'Tell him, Dave,' he said.

David felt a glow of pride at being called Dave.

'It's where they kill someone,' he said. 'Ain't it, Martin?'

Martin nodded and sipped the hot tea.

'What d'you mean?' said Kevin. 'I seen plenty of them.'

'No you ain't,' said Martin. 'They stopped 'em years back. You can't get 'em no more. 'Cept if you know how.'

'I seen all sorts,' said Kevin. 'I seen *Forest of Blood* and *Sawmill*. You seen *Sawmill*?'

'That ain't a snuff movie. You're a berk, you are. This is real. There's someone really killed on this. You see it being done. You ain't never seen that.'

David again felt his stomach lift. He hoped desperately that he wouldn't be sick in front of Martin when the time came. Even thinking about it . . .

'There's that kid again,' said Kevin.

He pointed to the brightly-lit doorway of an electricity board showroom opposite. Sandwich-makers, microwave ovens, cookers, heaters, freezers, and in the doorway gazing in, the thin huddled figure from the car. As they looked he wandered away from there and stared through the window of the supermarket next door.

Martin looked away.

'If you're scared, you needn't watch it,' he said.

'Course I ain't scared,' said Kevin. 'I seen *Sawmill* and I weren't scared of that.'

'This is different,' said Martin.

David looked out of the window again, but the other boy had gone.

Martin turned the key and opened the door. The house was full of darkness and the smell of chips and tobacco smoke. David felt the warmth on his cheeks. He'd never been to Martin's house before, and he looked around curiously as Martin put the hall light on. There was a really smart carpet, and a mirror with all gold round it, and a TV phone. He felt reassured. It was so nice that you couldn't imagine anything horrible happening there. *Snuff Park* might not be all that bad. And he could always close his eyes.

'You going to put it on then?' said Kevin. 'Where's the telly?'

'No hurry. I want something to eat first. Ain't you hungry?'

'What you got to eat?'

'Dunno. Fish and chips'll do. You better eat it now 'cause you won't want to after, will he, Dave?'

'No,' said David. 'Not after.'

'Here,' said Martin to David, handing him a ten-pound note. 'Go round the chippy. Cod and chips three times, all right?'

'Ta, Martin,' said David, and added 'Don't start it without me.'

The chip shop was just around the corner. On his way back, with the soft hot bundles clutched to his chest, David suddenly stopped. The boy from the car was standing outside Martin's front door.

'What do you want?' said David, before he could stop himself.

'You going to watch the video?' said the boy.

David could hardly hear what he said. He supposed the boy had got a cold, or asthma, like David's sister.

'Yeah,' he said.

'Can I watch it?'

'I dunno. It ain't mine, it's my mate's.'

The two boys stood still, not looking at each other.

'I'll ask him,' said David finally, and rang the bell.

When Martin opened the door David said 'I got 'em. Three cod and chips. And this kid was there outside the house. He says he wants to watch the video.'

Martin twisted his mouth. Kevin, behind him, said, 'He'll never take it. He'll never take the pressure.'

'All right, let's see if he does,' said Martin. 'Let him in, then.'

The strange boy came in after David and stood in the living-room while they ate their fish and chips. David offered him some, but he just said, 'No, I don't want none.' After a minute or two he sat down. The others didn't say anything, but ate quickly, and dropped their papers in the fireplace. David could smell the strange boy again. The room was hot, and he dropped his anorak on the thick red carpet, but the strange boy kept his on, and sat with his hands in his pockets, unmoving.

'All right then?' said Martin. 'I'll put it on.'

He fitted the cassette into the machine and sprawled back in a big leather armchair with the remote control. David and Kevin were sitting on the settee, and the other boy was on a dining chair by the table. Martin turned the TV on.

'Smart telly,' said Kevin.

It was a 48-inch. The big screen lifted itself out of the console and filled with colour.

'You seen a snuff picture before?' said Martin to the strange boy.

'Yeah. I seen this one.' They had to strain to hear him.

'This one?' It was plain that Martin didn't believe him. 'You know what happens?'

'Yeah. I seen it hundreds of times.'

'Hundreds? Get lost.'

'Here,' said Kevin. 'Let's watch it with the light out.'

'Stay there,' said Martin. 'Watch this.'

He pressed a button on the remote control, and the big centre light above them faded into darkness. Now the only light came from the screen.

'Smart!' said Kevin.

They found themselves watching a suburban street from the windscreen of a moving car. It was a sunny day. There were lots of trees covered in leaves, and the houses looked nice and big, with lots of space between them.

Then the commentary began.

'Just an ordinary road in an ordinary English town,' said a man's voice. It was a strong deep voice, warm and concerned. 'An ordinary summer's day. But for one woman nothing will be the same again. There will never be another summer's day for her.'

David looked at the strange boy. His eyes were wide and fixed intently on the screen, and his lips were moving unconsciously with the words. David felt queer. He knew now very strongly that he didn't want to watch the film at all. He let his eyes go back to the screen, but tried to make them out of focus so that he couldn't see clearly.

A few minutes passed. There was no more commentary from the film, but suddenly the strange boy said something.

'What?' said Martin.

'I says it's a nice house, ain't it?' said the boy.

Kevin, frowning concentratedly, took no notice. Martin grunted, but David looked at the boy again. Anything to get his eyes off the screen; but nothing had happened yet.

'Must be nice living there,' said the boy, still staring. But his expression was strange; David couldn't understand it.

'Yeah,' he said to the boy.

There was a woman on the screen. She was doing normal things, like washing up and ironing. She was talking to the camera about housework or something. David felt full of fear, almost ready to be sick, because it was all so ordinary, and you knew she was real, and you knew it had really happened, like this, and you knew you were going to see her murdered.

'This is boring,' said Kevin. 'What's she on about?'

'Shut up,' said Martin. 'They got the camera in there to get her confidence.'

'But there ain't nothing happening,' said Kevin. 'She's just bloody talking.'

'She's pretty, ain't she?' said the boy.

The other two fell silent, and turned to him for a moment. Even David sensed it was an odd thing to say.

'Eh?' said Martin.

'I says she's pretty, ain't she. She's really nice.'

'What d'you mean?' said Kevin.

'She's my mum,' said the boy.

There was another silence then. Everything had suddenly changed, and David felt it, but didn't know how or why.

'Eh?' said Martin.

'I says she's my mum. She loves me and I love her.'

The boys shifted in their seats. The pictures on the screen had changed. It was night-time, and the camera was outside the house looking in through the kitchen window. The room was warmly lit; the woman was moving about, alone, watering some big green plants. She bent down and picked up a little baby from what must have been a carry-cot, and cuddled it. But none of the three boys were taking this in: they were paralysed by what the strange boy had said. No-one said that sort of thing.

'He's mad,' said Kevin uneasily.

'Hey, what's your name?' said Martin.

There was no reply. Instead the commentary began again:

'Alone. There is no-one to help. Little does she know that an unseen hand has cut the phone wire. And now . . . the fear begins.'

The boy was mouthing the words as if he knew them by heart. Suddenly from the darkness a stone shattered the kitchen window, and the woman gasped and turned wildly, clutching the baby to her. Her wide-eyed face stared out at them, and then they all saw at once that she *was* his mother.

She was bending now, putting the baby down swiftly. And then another window shattered, and she jumped and cried out.

David's heart was beating like a captured bird.

'Martin –' he started to say, but Martin himself spoke at the same time, loudly, sitting up tensely in his chair and turning to the strange boy.

'What d'you want?' he cried. 'What you come here for?'

Kevin was shifting himself next to David, making himself look small and inconspicuous, like he did in class. Martin's face was twisted and full of hate.

'Just wanted to see –' began the strange boy, but his dry rustling voice was drowned by a scream from the TV. David flicked a sideways look at the screen: a man with a stocking mask had burst into the kitchen. There was a blur in the sound, as if two pieces of film had been joined carelessly, and then the camera was suddenly inside the kitchen with them.

'Martin!' cried David.

'What's the matter?' shouted Martin. He was shaking, glaring at the screen, staring wildly, gripping the remote control. 'You scared? You seen enough?' He pressed the volume switch, and terrible sounds flooded the room. David put his hands over his ears. Kevin was still watching, but he'd curled up very small, and he was holding his fists in front of his mouth.

And the strange boy was still gazing at the screen. The woman was speaking, gabbling desperately, and the boy's eyes followed her and his lips moved with her words.

'Shut up!' Martin yelled. 'Shut up!'

He jumped up and dropped the remote control. The picture faded at once, and the last thing David saw was Martin's face, wet with sweat.

They were in darkness.

No one moved.

David heard Martin gulping and breathing heavily. He felt sick with fear and shame.

The strange boy said, 'It ain't finished.'

'Shut up!' said Martin fiercely. 'Get out!'

'I can't till it's finished. I always see the end.'

'What you want to watch it for?'

'I always watch it. That's the only time I see her. I like seeing my mum.'

In the darkness his voice sounded more than ever distant, and cold, and strange. David's skin was crawling. Everything was horrible. It had been horrible all day, but this was worse than anything. He thought of his own mum, and nearly sobbed out loud, but stifled it just in time.

'And the baby.' The strange boy spoke again. 'It's a nice baby, ain't it? It looks nice. It must be nice being picked up like that, like what she does. I wish I could remember.'

'What d'you mean?' said Martin hoarsely.

The boy's voice was even quieter now: hardly more than dead leaves falling.

'They killed her and then they set fire to the house. It all burnt up, the baby and all. That was me, that was, that baby. I burnt up all with my mum. But I didn't stop growing up, getting older, like. It must be the video. Sort of kept me going. I seen it hundreds of times. The best bit is where she picks me up. I reckon she must have loved me a lot. That's all I do, watch that video. There ain't nothing else . . .'

He stopped.

Martin stumbled to the door and felt for the light-switch. The room sprang into being around them, all solid and bright, but there was no-one else there. Only a sharp, distant smell remained, and that dwindled after a moment and then vanished completely as if it had never existed. The boy was gone.

*   *   *

PHILIP PULLMAN is the author of the controversial, best-selling trilogy, *His Dark Materials* – the first book of which which has earned him the Carnegie Medal, the *Guardian*'s Fiction Award and the British Best Award. Then in 2001 the final part won him the coveted Whitbread 'Book of the Year' beating Ian Rankin, Jacqueline Wilson and even Harry Potter's creator, J.K.Rowling. His fantastically inventive trilogy runs to 1,300 pages and features two very single-minded teenagers, Will and Lyra, and their quest to save the world. The books include visions of the grey land of the dead, a tyranically run Heaven and the death of God. Although some critics have accused *His Dark Materials* of being 'the stuff of nightmares', Philip resolutely defends himself and his work: 'Children's books are the only place where really great writing can happen,' he says.

Born in Norwich, the author was a schoolteacher in Oxford for twenty years, which provided him with a special insight into the minds of children and has made his fiction increasingly popular. His books range from a sequence of Victorian adventures, which include *The Ruby in the Smoke* (1985) to a thriller, *The White Mercedes* (1992) (reissued as *The Butterfly Tattoo* in 1998) set in contemporary Oxford. Major acclaim came for his brilliant trilogy which began with *Northern Lights* (1995), continued in *The Subtle Knife* (1997) and has just been completed by the award-winning *The Amber Spyglass* (2001). Like another famous writer for young readers, Roald

Dahl, Philip Pullman works in a shed in his garden where he reckons to write 1,100 words a day. 'Video Nasty' is a chilling example of his remarkable story-telling skills, which might just scare adults even more than kids!

THE HOUSE OF NO RETURN

R.L. Stine

*There are also three friends in this story – Robbie, Nathan
and Lori. They've formed the Danger Club. The only way to
get in is to spend an hour in the old, decaying house on
Willow Hill. No one has lived there for years and everyone
believes it is haunted. Now, Robbie, Nathan and Lori have
never themselves actually been in the building with its spots
of red brick showing through the peeling white paint like
bloodstains. But they do need more members. After having
no luck with the wimp, Doug, the three pick on Chris
Wakely, a shy boy, new to the town. When he also refuses, the
group decide to try to trick him inside on Hallowe'en night.
But their trick-or-treating soon runs the danger of not just
being scary but of actually scaring them to death.*

*   *   *

We were afraid to go too close to the house. So we
stayed down at the street, staring up at it. Staring
across the bare, sloping front garden.

No grass would grow in that garden. The trees,
gnarled and bent, were all dead. Not even weeds
sprouted in the dry, cracked dirt.

At the top of the sloping garden, the house
seemed to stare back at us. The two upstairs windows
gaped like two unblinking black eyes.

The house was wide and solid-looking. Built of bricks. Many years ago, the bricks had been painted white. But now the paint was faded and peeling. Spots of red brick showed through like bloodstains.

The window shutters were cracked. Several had fallen off. The beams of the front porch tilted dangerously. A strong wind could blow the porch over.

No one lived there. The house had been empty for years and years.

No one *could* live there.

The house was haunted. Everyone in town said it was.

Everyone knew the legend of the house: if you spent the night inside it, you would never come out.

That's why we brought kids there. That's why we dared them to go inside.

You couldn't join our Danger Club unless you stayed inside the house – by yourself – for an hour.

Staring up at the house, bathed in a haze of pale moonlight, I shivered. I zipped my wind-breaker up to my chin and crossed my arms over my chest.

'How long has he been in there, Robbie?' Nathan asked me.

Lori and I both raised our wrists to check our watches. 'Only ten minutes,' I told Nathan.

'Fifty minutes to go,' Lori said. 'Think he'll make it?'

'Doug is pretty brave,' I replied thoughtfully, watching the moon disappear behind a cloud. 'He might last another five minutes!' I said, grinning.

Lori and Nathan sniggered.

The three of us felt safe down here by the street.

Poor Doug probably didn't feel too safe right now. He was shut inside the dark house. Trying to stay there an hour so he could join our club.

I turned and saw a light rolling silently over the street, coming towards us. A white, ghostly light.

My breath caught in my throat.

It's a car, I realized, as it floated closer. A car with only one headlight. The first car we'd seen on this street all night.

The beam from the headlight washed over my two friends and me, forcing us to shield our eyes. As it passed, we turned back to the house – and heard a shrill scream.

A wail of terror.

'Here he comes!' Nathan cried.

Sure enough, Doug burst out through the front door. He stumbled off the crumbling porch and came tearing across the dead, bare garden.

His hands waved wildly in front of him. His head was tilted back, and his mouth was frozen open in one long, high shriek of fright.

'Doug – what did you see?' I called. 'Did you really see a ghost?'

'S-something touched my *face*!' he wailed. He ran right past Nathan, Lori and me, screaming his head off.

'Probably only a spider's web,' I murmured.

'Robbie – we've got to stop him!' Lori cried.

'Doug! Hey – Doug!' We called his name and

chased after him, our trainers slapping loudly on the pavement.

Waving his arms frantically and screaming, leaning into the wind, Doug kept running.

We couldn't catch him. 'He'll run home,' I said breathlessly. I stopped and leaned over, pressing my hands against my knees, trying to catch my breath.

Up ahead, we could still hear poor Doug's frightened wail.

'Guess he doesn't join the club,' I said, still breathing hard.

'What do we do now?' Nathan asked, glancing back at the house.

'I guess we find another victim,' I replied.

Chris Wakely seemed like a perfect victim.

His family had moved to town last summer, and Chris started in my sixth-grade class in September. Chris had pale blue eyes and very short, white-blond hair. He was a bit shy, but he seemed like a really nice guy.

One day after school, I saw Chris walking home and I hurried to catch up with him. It was a windy October day. All around us, red and yellow leaves were falling from the trees. It looked as if it was raining leaves.

I said hi to Chris and started telling him about our club. I asked if he'd like to join.

'It's only for brave people,' I explained. 'In order to join, you have to spend an hour at night inside the house on Willow Hill.'

Chris stopped walking and turned to me, squinting at me with those pale blue eyes. 'Isn't that house supposed to be haunted?' he asked.

I laughed. 'You don't believe in ghosts – do you?'

He didn't smile. His expression turned serious. The light seemed to fade in his eyes. 'I'm not very brave,' he said softly.

We started to walk again. Our trainers crunched on the leaves strewn over the pavement. 'We'd really like you to join the club,' I told him. 'You're brave enough to spend one hour in an empty house, aren't you?'

He shrugged and lowered his eyes. 'I – I don't think so,' he stammered. 'I've always been afraid of monsters and things,' he admitted. 'I believed there was a monster living under my bed until I was eight!'

I laughed. But his expression remained solemn. He wasn't kidding.

'When I go to a scary movie,' Chris continued, 'I have to duck under the seat when the scary parts come on.'

Lori and Nathan came running up to us. 'Are you going to do it?' Nathan asked Chris. 'Are you going to join the club?'

Chris shoved his hands deep into his jeans pockets. 'Did you guys spend an hour in the house?' he asked.

I shook my head. 'We don't have to,' I told him. 'We started the club, so we don't have to go in the house. We already know we like danger. New members have to prove themselves.'

Chris chewed thoughtfully at his lower lip. We turned the corner and kept walking. The house was up the hill, at the end of the block.

We stopped in front of it and stared across the bare front garden. 'See? It doesn't look scary at all in the daytime,' I said.

Chris swallowed hard. 'Needs a paint job,' he muttered. 'And how come all the trees died?'

'No one to take care of them,' Nathan said. 'How about it, Chris?' I urged. 'We really need new members.'

'Yeah,' Lori agreed. 'A club isn't much fun with only three kids in it.'

Chris had his eyes on the house. He kept his hands jammed into his jeans pockets. I thought I saw him shiver. But it might have been the wind rustling his jacket.

'W-will you come in with me?' he asked.

'No way,' I replied, shaking my head.

'We can't,' Lori told him. 'The idea of the club is to show how brave you are.'

'We won't come in,' Nathan said. 'But we'll wait outside for you.'

'Come on, Chris,' I urged. 'Do it. It'll be fun! It's almost Halloween. Get in the spirit!'

He swallowed a couple of times, staring up at the house. Then he shook his head. 'I really don't want to,' he murmured in a low voice, so low I could barely hear him. 'Guess I'm a bit of a scaredy-cat.'

I started to plead with him. But I could see he was really embarrassed. So I didn't say any more.

Chris waved goodbye and hurried off towards his house. Lori, Nathan and I watched him until he disappeared around the corner.

'Now what?' Nathan asked.

We held a club meeting at my house two nights later. It was a pretty boring meeting. None of us could think of another cool kid to join our club. And we couldn't think of anything fun to do.

'Halloween is Saturday,' I moaned. 'We should be able to think of something scary to do.'

'What are you going to dress up as?' Lori asked Nathan.

'Freddy Krueger,' Nathan replied. 'I've already bought the metal fingernails.'

'Weren't you Freddy Krueger last year?' I asked him.

'So? I *like* being Freddy Krueger!' Nathan insisted.

'You and every other kid in school,' Lori muttered.

Lori planned to dress as a vampire. And I had my monster costume all ready.

'We need more club members,' Lori said, sighing. 'You can't have a club with just three people.'

'Chris would be perfect,' I replied. 'If only he weren't such a scaredy-cat.'

'You know,' Nathan started, rubbing his chin thoughtfully, 'it would be really good for Chris to get over his fears.'

'Huh? What do you mean?' I asked.

'I mean we could help Chris out,' Nathan replied, smiling. 'We could help him be brave.'

I still didn't understand. 'Nathan – what are you saying?'

His smile grew wider. 'We could *force* him to go into the house.'

I called Chris later that night and invited him to go trick-or-treating with us. He said yes. He sounded grateful to have some kids to go around with. He had only been at our school two months, and he hadn't made many friends.

The three of us met at my house on Halloween. Nathan clicked his long metal nails and kept cackling and grinning like Freddy Kreuger. I was a very cool monster, with eyeballs on springs popping from my purple head. Lori kept talking in a weird vampire voice.

'Where's Chris?' Nathan asked, looking around. 'Is he meeting us here?'

'Yeah. Where is he?' Lori demanded.

We were all a little tense. We were playing a mean trick on Chris. But we knew he'd feel good about things by the end of the night.

The doorbell rang, and we all ran to answer it. Chris stood in the porch light, his face an ugly green. He raised both hands to show them to us. They were covered in green, too.

'What are *you* supposed to be – a pea pod?' I joked.

Chris looked hurt. 'No. I'm a corpse.'

'Very scary,' I said. I handed out trick-or-treat bags. 'Let's get going.' I led the way down the driveway and up the street.

We stopped at several houses and collected sweets. It was a cool, windy night with a tiny sliver of a moon. Gusts of wind kept fluttering our costumes and making our trick-or-treat bags fly up.

We were approaching the house on Willow Hill. I had a heavy feeling in my stomach. My hands suddenly felt ice cold.

I hope Chris can stay in the house for a whole hour, I thought. He's such a nice guy. I'd really like him to be in the club.

Such a nice guy. And we were about to do such a mean thing to him.

But he'll quickly get over it, I told myself. And he'll be glad we made him test his bravery.

The eerie house came into view. I saw Chris glance at it, then quickly turn to cross the street. He didn't want to go near it. Especially on Halloween night.

But Nathan and I grabbed him by the arms. Chris cried out in surprise. 'Hey – let go! What are you guys doing?'

Chris struggled to pull free. But Nathan and I were much bigger than him, and stronger.

Lori led the way over the bare, dirt garden, up the sloping hill to the dark, silent house. Chris tried to swing both arms, tried desperately to break free. But Nathan and I dragged him on to the tilting porch, up to the front door.

'No! Please!' Chris pleaded. 'Please – don't do this! Don't!'

I turned to him. Even under the green make-up, I could see the terror on his face. The poor guy was totally freaked!

'Chris, you'll be okay,' I said softly, soothingly. 'Go inside. It'll be fun. We'll wait for you. I promise.'

'You'll be proud of yourself,' Lori told him, helping to push him up to the door. 'And then you'll be in our club.'

Lori started to push open the heavy door. Nathan and I moved to shove Chris inside. But to my surprise, he reached out and grabbed my arm.

'Come in with me – please!' he begged, his eyes wide with fright. 'Please! I'm too scared! I'm just too scared!' He held on tightly to my arm. 'Let's all go in together – okay?'

I glanced at Lori and Nathan. 'No way,' I replied. 'You've got to prove your bravery, Chris. See you in an hour.'

We gave him a hard shove inside the house. Then we slammed the heavy door behind him.

'He seems so . . . scared,' Lori said, her voice muffled by the vampire fangs.

'He'll be okay,' I said. 'Let's wait for him down by the street.'

We took our places at the bottom of the driveway, and waited.

And waited.

We checked our watches after ten minutes. After twenty minutes. After half an hour.

'Chris is doing great!' I whispered, my eyes on the dark windows of the house. 'I didn't think he'd last *two* minutes.'

'He's a lot braver than I thought,' Nathan said from behind his Freddy Krueger mask.

We huddled close together, staring up at the house as the wind shook the trees all around us. Heavy clouds rolled over the moon, covering us in darkness.

We waited ten minutes more. Then ten minutes more.

'He's going to do it,' I said, checking my watch again. 'He's going to stay in there for a whole hour.'

'Let's really give him a big cheer when he comes out,' Lori suggested.

As the hour ended, we counted off the last thirty seconds out loud, one by one. Then we took a few steps up the driveway, eager to congratulate Chris and welcome him to the Danger Club.

But the front door didn't open. The house remained dark and silent.

Ten more minutes passed.

'I think he's showing off,' I said.

No one laughed. We kept our eyes raised to the house.

Ten more minutes. Then ten more.

'Where *is* he?' I cried shrilly.

'Something is wrong,' Lori said, taking the plastic vampire fangs out of her mouth. 'Something is wrong, Robbie.'

'Chris should be out of there by now,' Nathan agreed in a trembling voice.

I felt a chill run down my back. All of my muscles were tightening in dread. I knew my friends were right. Something bad had happened inside that house. Something very bad.

'We have to go in there,' Lori urged. 'We have to find Chris. We have to get him out.'

All three of us exchanged frightened glances. We didn't want to walk up that driveway. We didn't want to go inside that dark house.

But we didn't have a choice.

'Maybe we should wait a few more minutes,' I suggested, trying to stop my legs from shaking. 'Maybe he doesn't have a watch. Maybe he's–'

'Come on, Robbie.' Lori gave me a hard tug. 'Chris isn't coming out. We have to go and get him.'

The wind swirled around us, fluttering our costumes as we made our way up to the front door. I started to open the door, but my hand was so sweaty, the doorknob slid under my grasp.

Finally, Nathan and I pushed open the heavy door. The rusty hinges creaked as we opened the door and peered into the solid blackness.

'Chris?' I called. 'Chris you can come out now!' My voice sounded tiny and hollow.

No reply.

'Chris? Chris? Where are you?' All three of us began calling him.

The floor groaned and creaked beneath us as we took a few steps into the living room. The wind rattled the old window-panes.

'Chris – can you hear us? Chris?'

No reply.

A loud crash made all three of us cry out.

The front door had slammed behind us.

'J-just the wind, guys,' I choked out.

It was much darker with the door closed. But it didn't stay dark for long. Pale light flickered at the top of the stairs. It looked at first like dozens of fireflies clustered together.

I gasped as the light flared brighter. And floated down the stairs, like a shimmering cloud.

'Let's get out!' I cried.

Too late.

The shimmering cloud spread around us. And inside it I saw two frightening figures – a ghostly man and woman, hazy and transparent except for their red, glowing eyes.

Their terrifying eyes sparkled like fiery coals as they circled us, floating silently.

I can see right through both of them! I realized. This house really is haunted.

'Wh-where's Chris?' I managed to blurt out.

The man's voice was a dry whisper, the sound of wind through dead leaves. 'Your friend? He went out through the back door,' the ghost replied. 'About an hour ago.'

'We didn't want to let him go,' the woman whispered, her red eyes glowing brighter. 'But he made a bargain with us.' She sniggered, a dry, dead laugh. 'He promised that if we let him go, three kids would come in to take his place.'

'And here you are,' said the ghostly man, flashing an ugly, toothless smile. 'Here you are.'

'Don't look so frightened, kids,' the woman rasped, floating closer. 'You might as well make yourselves at home. You're all going to be here – *for ever*!'

*   *   *

R.L. STINE was declared in 2001 to be 'The Most Borrowed Children's Author' which means that an awful lot of kids have read his various novels in the *Goosebumps, Fear Street* and *Ghosts of Fear Street* series. It is reckoned that these books have sold over 300 million copies, putting him right up there as one of the top selling authors of all time. His stories in which children do all sorts of horrible things to one another – as well as to adults on lots of occasions – have also been made into a TV series called *Goosebumps*.

Like Philip Pullman, Robert Lawrence Stine was a junior school teacher, and it was his realisation just how much kids liked reading scary stories that inspired his first tales. He had always been a fan of the old horror comics and movies from the days of his childhood and this inspired his first novel, *The Baby Sitter* (1989) that became an immediate best-seller. Dozens of other writers have all tried to copy his terse style of writing, but none have enjoyed his enduring popularity. R.L. Stine claims – perhaps with a bit of tongue-in-cheek – that *everything* in his books has happened to him. 'You can't imagine what a horrifying life I've had!' he says. He won't say whether he still goes trick-or-treating on Hallowe'en – or whether any of his readers have tried to turn the tables on him. 'But I am proud when I get letters from kids who say they've actually screamed when reading one of my stories!'

LOST HEARTS

M.R. James

This next story, which takes place almost 200 years ago, is also about an old house – Aswarby Hall – although there is someone living there: a cranky old recluse called Mr Abney who has a reputation for disliking children. When Stephen, who is only twelve years old and has just lost his parents, is sent to live in the house, he is welcomed by the old man, but in a very creepy sort of way. All too soon the boy begins to realise that there is something very strange about Mr Abney and his house. He discovers that, years before, a little boy and girl also came to live here and disappeared under mysterious circumstances. Day by day, Stephen grows more scared that the same fate may be awaiting him . . .

*   *   *

It was, as far as I can ascertain, in September of the year 1811 that a postchaise drew up before the door of Aswarby Hall, in the heart of Lincolnshire. The little boy who was the only passenger in the chaise, and who jumped out as soon as it had stopped, looked about him with the keenest curiosity during the short interval that elapsed between the ringing of the bell and the opening of the hall door. He saw a tall, square, red-brick house, built in the reign of Anne ; a stone-pillared porch had been added in the purer classical style of 1790; the windows of the house were many, tall and narrow, with small panes and thick white woodwork. A pediment, pierced with a round window, crowned the front. There were wings to right and left, connected by curious glazed galleries, supported by colonnades, with the central block. These wings plainly cóntained the stables and offices of the house. Each was surmounted by an ornamental cupola with a gilded vane.

An evening light shone on the building, making the window-panes glow like so many fires. Away from the Hall in front stretched a flat park studded with oaks and fringed with firs, which stood out against the sky. The clock in the church-tower, buried in trees on the edge of the park, only its golden weather-cock catching the light, was striking six, and the sound came gently beating down the wind. It was altogether a pleasant impression, though tinged with the sort of melancholy appropriate to an evening in early autumn, that was conveyed to the mind of the boy who was standing in the porch waiting for the door to open to him.

He had just come from Warwickshire, and some six months ago had been left an orphan. Now, owing to the generous and unexpected offer of his elderly cousin, Mr. Abney, he had come to live at Aswarby. The offer was unexpected, because all who knew anything of Mr. Abney looked upon him as a some-what austere recluse, into whose steady-going house-hold the advent of a small boy would import a new and, it seemed, incongruous element. The truth is that very little was known of Mr. Abney's pursuits or temper. The Professor of Greek at Cambridge had been heard to say that no one knew more of the religious beliefs of the later pagans than did the owner of Aswarby. Certainly his library contained all the then available books bearing on the Mysteries, the Orphic poems, the worship of Mithras, and the Neo-Platonists. In the marble-paved hall stood a fine group of Mithras slaying a bull, which had been imported from the Levant at great expense by the owner. He had contributed a description of it to the *Gentleman's Magazine*, and he had written a remarkable series of articles in the *Critical Museum* on the superstitions of the Romans of the Lower Empire. He was looked upon, in fine, as a man wrapped up in his books, and it was a matter of great surprise among his neighbours that he should ever have heard of his orphan cousin, Stephen Elliott, much more that he should have volunteered to make him an inmate of Aswarby Hall.

Whatever may have been expected by his neighbours, it is certain that Mr. Abney – the tall, the thin, the austere – seemed inclined to give his young cousin a kindly reception. The moment the front-door was opened he darted out of his study, rubbing his hands with delight.

'How are you, my boy? – how are you? How old are you?' said he – 'that is, you are not too much tired, I hope, by your journey to eat your supper?'

'No, thank you, sir,' said Master Elliott; 'I am pretty well.'

'That's a good lad,' said Mr. Abney. 'And how old are you, my boy?'

It seemed a little odd that he should have asked the question twice in the first two minutes of their acquaintance.

'I'm twelve years old next birthday, sir,' said Stephen.

'And when is your birthday, my dear boy? Eleventh of September, eh? That's well – that's very well. Nearly a year hence, isn't it? I like – ha, ha! – I like to get these things down in my book. Sure it's twelve? Certain?'

'Yes, quite sure, sir.'

'Well, well! Take him to Mrs. Bunch's room, Parkes, and let him have his tea – supper – whatever it is.'

'Yes, sir,' answered the staid Mr. Parkes; and conducted Stephen to the lower regions.

Mrs. Bunch was the most comfortable and human person whom Stephen had as yet met in Aswarby. She made him completely at home; they were great friends in a quarter of an hour: and great friends they remained. Mrs. Bunch had been born in the neighbourhood some fifty-five years before the date of Stephen's arrival, and her residence at the Hall was of twenty years' standing. Consequently, if anyone knew the ins and outs of the house and the district, Mrs. Bunch knew them; and she was by no means disinclined to communicate her information.

Certainly there were plenty of things about the Hall and the Hall gardens which Stephen, who was of an adventurous and inquiring turn, was anxious to have explained to him. 'Who built the temple at the end of the laurel walk? Who was the old man whose picture hung on the staircase, sitting at a table, with a skull under his hand?' These and many similar points were cleared up by the resources of Mrs. Bunch's powerful intellect. There were others, however, of which the explanations furnished were less satisfactory.

One November evening Stephen was sitting by the fire in the housekeeper's room reflecting on his surroundings.

'Is Mr. Abney a good man, and will he go to heaven?' he suddenly asked, with the peculiar confidence which children possess in the ability of their elders to settle these questions, the decision of which is believed to be reserved for other tribunals.

'Good? – bless the child!' said Mrs. Bunch. 'Master's as kind a soul as ever I see! Didn't I never tell you of the little boy as he took in out of the street, as you may say, this seven years back? And the little girl, two years after I first come here?'

'No. Do tell me all about them, Mrs. Bunch – now this minute!'

'Well,' said Mrs. Bunch, 'the little girl I don't seem to recollect so much about. I know master brought her back with him from his walk one day, and give orders to Mrs. Ellis, as was housekeeper then, as she should be took every care with. And the pore child hadn't no one belonging to her – she told me so her own self – and here she lived with us a matter of three weeks it might be; and then, whether she were somethink of a gipsy in her blood or what not, but one morning she out of her bed afore any of us had opened a eye, and neither track nor yet trace of her have I set eyes on since. Master was wonderful put about, and had all the ponds dragged; but it's my belief she was had away by them gipsies, for there was singing round the house for as much as an hour the night she went, and Parkes, he declare as he heard them a-calling in the woods all that afternoon. Dear, dear! An odd child she was, so silent in her ways and all, but I was wonderful taken up with her, so domesticated she was – surprising.'

'And what about the little boy?' said Stephen.

'Ah, that pore boy!' sighed Mrs. Bunch. 'He were a foreigner – Jevanny he called hisself – and he come a-tweaking his 'urdy-gurdy round and about the drive one winter day, and master 'ad him in that minute, and ast all about where he came from, and how old he was, and how he made his way, and where was his relatives, and all as kind as heart could wish. But it went the same way with him. They're a hunruly lot, them foreign nations, I do suppose, and he was off one fine morning just the same as the girl. Why he went and what he done was our question for as much as a year after; for he never took his 'urdy-gurdy, and there it lays on the shelf.'

The remainder of the evening was spent by Stephen in miscellaneous cross-examination of Mrs. Bunch and in efforts to extract a tune from the hurdy-gurdy.

That night he had a curious dream. At the end of the passage at the top of the house, in which his bedroom was situated, there was an old disused bathroom. It was kept locked, but the upper half of the door was glazed, and, since the muslin curtains which used to hang there had long been gone, you could look in and see the lead-lined bath affixed to the wall on the right hand, with its head towards the window.

On the night of which I am speaking, Stephen Elliott found himself, as he thought, looking through the glazed door. The moon was shining through the window, and he was gazing at a figure which lay in the bath.

His description of what he saw reminds me of what I once beheld myself in the famous vaults of St. Michan's Church in Dublin, which possess the horrid property of preserving corpses from decay for centuries. A figure inexpressibly thin and pathetic, of a dusty leaden colour, enveloped in a shroud-like garment, the thin lips crooked into a faint and dreadful smile, the hands pressed tightly over the region of the heart.

As he looked upon it, a distant, almost inaudible moan seemed to issue from its lips, and the arms began to stir. The terror of the sight forced Stephen backwards, and he awoke to the fact that he was indeed standing on the cold boarded floor of the passage in the full light of the moon. With a courage which I do not think can be common among boys of his age, he went to the door of the bathroom to ascertain if the figure of his dream were really there. It was not, and he went back to bed.

Mrs. Bunch was much impressed next morning by his story, and went so far as to replace the muslin curtain over the glazed door of the bathroom. Mr. Abney, moreover, to whom he confided his experiences at breakfast, was greatly interested, and made notes of the matter in what he called 'his book.'

The spring equinox was approaching, as Mr. Abney frequently reminded his cousin, adding that this had been always considered by the ancients to be a critical time for the young: that Stephen would do well to take care of himself, and to shut his bedroom window at night; and that Censorinus had some valuable remarks on the subject. Two incidents that occurred about this time made an impression upon Stephen's mind.

The first was after an unusually uneasy and oppressed night that he had passed – though he could not recall any particular dream that he had had.

The following evening Mrs. Bunch was occupying herself in mending his nightgown.

'Gracious me, Master Stephen!' she broke forth rather irritably, 'how do you manage to tear your nightdress all to flinders this way? Look here, sir, what trouble you do give to poor servants that have to darn and mend after you!'

There was indeed a most destructive and apparently wanton series of slits or scorings in the garment, which would undoubtedly require a skilful needle to make good. They were confined to the left side of the chest – long, parallel slits, about six inches in length, some of them not quite piercing the texture of the linen. Stephen could only express his entire ignorance of their origin: he was sure they were not there the night before.

'But,' he said, 'Mrs. Bunch, they are just the same as the scratches on the outside of my bedroom door; and I'm sure I never had anything to do with making *them*.'

Mrs. Bunch gazed at him open-mouthed, then snatched up a candle, departed hastily from the room, and was heard making her way upstairs. In a few minutes she came down.

'Well,' she said, 'Master Stephen, it's a funny thing to me how them marks and scratches can 'a' come there – too high up for any cat or dog to 'ave made 'em, much less a rat: for all the world like a Chinaman's fingernails, as my uncle in the tea-trade used to tell us of when we was girls together. I wouldn't say nothing to master, not if I was you, Master Stephen, my dear; and just turn the key of the door when you go to your bed.'

'I always do, Mrs. Bunch, as soon as I've said my prayers.'

'Ah, that's a good child: always say your prayers, and then no one can't hurt you.'

Herewith Mrs. Bunch addressed herself to mending the injured nightgown, with intervals of meditation, until bed-time. This was on a Friday night in March, 1812.

On the following evening the usual duet of
Stephen and Mrs. Bunch was augmented by the
sudden arrival of Mr. Parkes, the butler, who as a rule
kept himself rather *to* himself in his own pantry. He
did not see that Stephen was there: he was, moreover,
flustered and less slow of speech than was his wont.

'Master may get up his own wine, if he likes, of an
evening,' was his first remark. 'Either I do it in the
daytime or not at all, Mrs. Bunch. I don't know what
it may be: very like it's the rats, or the wind got into
the cellars; but I'm not so young as I was, and I can't
go through with it as I have done.'

'Well, Mr. Parkes, you know it is a surprising place
for the rats, is the Hall.'

'I'm not denying that, Mrs. Bunch; and, to be sure,
many a time I've heard the tale from the men in the
shipyards about the rat that could speak. I never laid
no confidence in that before; but to-night, if I'd
demeaned myself to lay my ear to the door of the
further bin, I could pretty much have heard what
they was saying.'

'Oh, there, Mr. Parkes, I've no patience with your
fancies! Rats talking in the wine-cellar indeed!'

'Well, Mrs. Bunch, I've no wish to argue with you:
all I say is, if you choose to go to the far bin, and lay
your ear to the door, you may prove my words this
minute.'

'What nonsense you do talk, Mr. Parkes – not fit for
children to listen to! Why, you'll be frightening
Master Stephen there out of his wits.'

'What! Master Stephen?' said Parkes, awaking to

the consciousness of the boy's presence. 'Master Stephen knows well enough when I'm a-playing a joke with you, Mrs. Bunch.'

In fact, Master Stephen knew much too well to suppose that Mr. Parkes had in the first instance intended a joke. He was interested, not altogether pleasantly, in the situation; but all his questions were unsuccessful in inducing the butler to give any more detailed account of his experiences in the wine-cellar.

We have now arrived at March 24, 1812. It was a day of curious experiences for Stephen: a windy, noisy day, which filled the house and the gardens with a restless impression. As Stephen stood by the fence of the grounds, and looked out into the park, he felt as if an endless procession of unseen people were sweeping past him on the wind, borne on resistlessly and aimlessly, vainly striving to stop themselves, to catch at something that might arrest their flight and bring them once again into contact with the living world of which they had formed a part. After luncheon that day Mr. Abney said:

'Stephen, my boy, do you think you could manage to come to me to-night as late as eleven o'clock in my study? I shall be busy until that time, and I wish to show you something connected with your future life which it is most important that you should know. You are not to mention this matter to Mrs. Bunch nor to anyone else in the house; and you had better go to your room at the usual time.'

Here was a new excitement added to life: Stephen eagerly grasped at the opportunity of sitting up till eleven o'clock. He looked in at the library door on his way upstairs that evening, and saw a brazier, which he had often noticed in the corner of the room, moved out before the fire; an old silver-gilt cup stood on the table, filled with red wine, and some written sheets of paper lay near it. Mr. Abney was sprinkling some incense on the brazier from a round silver box as Stephen passed, but did not seem to notice his step.

The wind had fallen, and there was a still night and a full moon. At about ten o'clock Stephen was standing at the open window of his bedroom, looking out over the country. Still as the night was, the mysterious population of the distant moonlit woods was not yet lulled to rest. From time to time strange cries as of lost and despairing wanderers sounded from across the mere. They might be the notes of owls or water-birds, yet they did not quite resemble either sound. Were not they coming nearer? Now they sounded from the nearer side of the water, and in a few moments they seemed to be floating about among the shrubberies. Then they ceased; but just as Stephen was thinking of shutting the window and resuming his reading of 'Robinson Crusoe,' he caught sight of two figures standing on the gravelled terrace that ran along the garden side of the Hall – the figures of a boy and girl, as it seemed; they stood side by side, looking up at the windows. Something in the form of the girl recalled irresistibly his dream of the figure in the bath. The boy inspired him with more acute fear.

Whilst the girl stood still, half smiling, with her hands clasped over her heart, the boy, a thin shape, with black hair and ragged clothing, raised his arms in the air with an appearance of menace and of unappeasable hunger and longing. The moon shone upon his almost transparent hands, and Stephen saw that the nails were fearfully long and that the light shone through them. As he stood with his arms thus raised, he disclosed a terrifying spectacle. On the left side of his chest there opened a black and gaping rent; and there fell upon Stephen's brain, rather than upon his ear, the impression of one of those hungry and desolate cries that he had heard resounding over the woods of Aswarby all that evening. In another moment this dreadful pair had moved swiftly and noiselessly over the dry gravel, and he saw them no more.

Inexpressibly frightened as he was, he determined to take his candle and go down to Mr. Abney's study, for the hour appointed for their meeting was near at hand. The study or library opened out of the front-hall on one side, and Stephen, urged on by his terrors, did not take long in getting there. To effect an entrance was not so easy. It was not locked, he felt sure, for the key was on the outside of the door as usual. His repeated knocks produced no answer. Mr. Abney was engaged: he was speaking. What! why did he try to cry out? and why was the cry choked in his throat? Had he, too, seen the mysterious children?

But now everything was quiet, and the door yielded to Stephen's terrified and frantic pushing.

On the table in Mr. Abney's study certain papers were found which explained the situation to Stephen Elliott when he was of an age to understand them. The most important sentences were as follows:

'It was a belief very strongly and generally held by the ancients – of whose wisdom in these matters I have had such experience as induces me to place confidence in their assertions – that by enacting certain processes, which to us moderns have something of a barbaric complexion, a very remarkable enlightenment of the spiritual faculties in man may be attained: that, for example, by absorbing the personalities of a certain number of his fellow-creatures, an individual may gain a complete ascendancy over those orders of spiritual beings which control the elemental forces of our universe.

'It is recorded of Simon Magus that he was able to fly in the air, to become invisible, or to assume any form he pleased, by the agency of the soul of a boy whom, to use the libellous phrase employed by the author of the "Clementine Recognitions," he had "murdered." I find it set-down, moreover, with considerable detail in the writings of Hermes Trismegistus, that similar happy results may be produced by the absorptions of the hearts of not less than three human beings below the age of twenty-one years. To the testing of the truth of this receipt I have devoted the greater part of the last twenty years, selecting as the *corpora vilia* of my experiment such persons as could conveniently be removed without occasioning a sensible gap in society. The first step I effected by the removal of one Phœbe Stanley, a girl of gipsy extraction, on March 24, 1792. The second, by the removal of a wandering Italian lad, named Giovanni Paoli, on the night of March 23, 1805. The final "victim" – to employ a word repugnant in the highest degree to my feelings – must be my cousin, Stephen Elliott. His day must be this March 24, 1812.

'The best means of effecting the required absorption is to remove the heart from the *living* subject, to reduce it to ashes, and to mingle them with about a pint of some red wine, preferably port. The remains of the first two subjects, at least, it will be well to conceal: a disused bath-room or wine-cellar will be found convenient for such a purpose. Some annoyance may be experienced from the psychic portion of the subjects, which popular language dignifies with the name of ghosts. But the man of philosophic temperament – to whom alone the experiment is appropriate – will be little prone to attach importance to the feeble efforts of these beings to wreak their vengeance on him. I contemplate with the liveliest satisfaction the enlarged and emancipated existence which the experiment, if successful, will confer on me; not only placing me beyond the reach of human justice (so-called), but eliminating to a great extent the prospect of death itself.'

Mr. Abney was found in his chair, his head thrown back, his face stamped with an expression of rage, fright, and mortal pain. In his left side was a terrible lacerated wound, exposing the heart. There was no blood on his hands, and a long knife that lay on the table was perfectly clean. A savage wild-cat might have inflicted the injuries. The window of the study was open, and it was the opinion of the coroner that Mr. Abney had met his death by the agency of some wild creature. But Stephen Elliott's study of the papers I have quoted led him to a very different conclusion.

*   *   *

M.R. JAMES is one of the most famous writers of ghost stories in the world and although many of his tales were created in the early years of the twentieth century, they have continued to thrill new generations of readers ever since. The first collection of his work, *Ghost Stories of an Antiquary*, was published in 1904 and many of the tales have subsequently been broadcast on the radio, adapted for television or made into films, such as 'Casting the Runes' (1911) about the persecution of an old professor by a black magician trying to raise evil demons, which was made into the cult movie, *Curse of the Demon* (1957).

Montague Rhodes James was a teacher all his life (first at Cambridge and then Eton) and actually began writing supernatural stories to read to his friends at Christmas. These fireside ghost-story sessions became a tradition and it was his friends who encouraged him to get the tales published. Although he always gave the appearance of being a friendly and good-humoured man, M.R. James was perhaps

more nervous of the unknown than he let on –
though he did confess to one friend when asked if he
believed in ghosts: 'I am prepared to consider evidence and accept it if it satisfies me.' He had read
and enjoyed stories of the supernatural ever since his
own childhood and this, coupled with his life-long
association with young people, inspired him to feature children in some of his best stories like 'Lost
Hearts' which is believed to be partly based on a true
ghost story from Lincolnshire.

FINDERS KEEPERS

Anne McCaffrey

Peter has a special talent. He can 'find' anything. It enables him to turn up things like lost golf balls on the course near his home and then earn some cash by selling them back to the players. Peter is always a bit worried, though, that he will give away the secret of his skill – which would mean no money coming in to take care of his sick mother. She wants him to get an education and make a future for himself, but he loves her a lot and can't bear to see her suffer. The person he doesn't like is Ken Fargo, a manipulative insurance investigator with a flashy green Mustang, who is always creeping around his mother. And when Fargo forces Peter into helping him 'find' some valuable stolen furs, the boy's anxiety turns from worry to being really scared . . .

*   *   *

Peter turned in four dozen golf balls, including the monogrammed ones that Mr. Roche had been yelling about. The course manager was almost cheerful as he counted out Peter's finder's fee.

'You got a positive genius for scrounging balls, Pete. Don't know how you do it.'

'My mother says everyone's got something they're good at,' Peter replied and began to edge out the door of the stuffy office. Comments like that made him nervous: he half-expected he'd given away his secret and he and his mother'd be forced to run away again.

The manager grunted and muttered about keeping the members happy. Peter ducked out, running home with his pocketful of dollars. Mother'd be pleased although she didn't like him using his trick of 'finding' for 'material gain,' as she put it. Since she'd been so sick that she couldn't work at the diner, they'd precious little choice. Peter'd wanted to get a full time job as caddy but his mother had resisted.

'You can't be like me, Peter. You got to have education and training. Your father was a smart man but he hadn't enough education.' Her dedication made her eyes burn in her thin face. 'It's education that matters in this world, Peter. You got to go to school.' She emphasized that determination by stringing the words out and enunciating them clearly.

Peter adored his mother but he hated her attempts to imitate the 'country-club accents': her soft drawl and her habit of quoting country cliches only ruined the effect she wanted to project.

Seven dollars he was bringing home today. Not bad, added to the twenty-two he'd made on the weekend caddying. This week's rent, food and some of the medicine were now paid for. If he could just talk mother into letting him take a week off, now that the rains had stopped and spring sun was drying the greens, why he'd really make some money! Mr.

Roche always tipped a fiver, especially when Peter kept track of those monogrammed balls of his.

'Son, if you could patent that ball-homing instinct of yours,' Mr. Roche had said once, 'you'd be a millionaire!'

It'd made Peter almost scared to go caddying for Mr. Roche again but the money was too tempting.

He came around the corner of their bungalow and skidded to an abrupt stop in the mud by the hydrangeas. Ken Fargo's green Mustang was parked at the curb. The only good thing about his mother being sick was that she didn't have to be pleasant to creeps like Ken Fargo.

'He's pleasant enough and all that,' his mother had said and then shuddered, smiling quickly to reassure Peter. 'There's just something . . . slippery about him.' She sighed. 'I suppose he can't help being sour and suspicious. People do and say the most awful things to collect insurance! And he's lonely.'

His mother would understand being lonely, Peter thought. And she'd understand the awful things people do and say – particularly if you're any way different. But the knowledge hadn't made her sour, just more lonely and sad and cautious. Why she called his knack of finding things a gift, Peter didn't know. It was a curse! It'd brought them more grief, kept them moving about before he'd learn not to 'find' everything lost . . .

And why did Ken Fargo have to get unlost? They had thought him well gone when the insurance company he investigated called off the search for the hijacked furs. There was a reward of $15,000 for the return of those coats. Try as he would, Peter couldn't figure a legitimate way to 'find' those furs. He hadn't been with the searchers when they'd looked in the old lead mine, or he'd have 'found' the furs under the concealing layer of rubble in the ore carts. He couldn't go there alone. That old shaft was dangerous, the supports worm-ridden and damp-rotted. Every kid in town had been warned, on pain of a strapping, to stay away.

Peter paused at the front of the house. He didn't want to go in. He didn't like the way Ken Fargo looked at his mother and there wasn't much a thirteen year old boy could do to a six-foot man who'd fought his way out of some nasty corners (Fargo's words) and *looked* it from the scars on his face and knuckles. Peter took a deep breath and stomped up the three steps.

Peter knew the moment he walked into the room that Fargo had been badgering his mother. She was flushed and wringing her hands.

'Peter!' she all but swooped down on him. 'Did you have a good day?' She was terribly relieved to see him.

'Sure did, mother.' He held out the seven dollar bills. 'Hello, Mr. Fargo.' He had to acknowledge the man's presence or his mother would chew him out for bad manners no matter how much she disliked Fargo.

'Long time no see,' the man replied, jerking his shoulders to settle the flashy gold sports jacket. He sauntered towards the window. 'Sorry your ma's been ill. Should've let me know.'

Peter blinked at him in surprise.

'Seven dollars,' his mother was saying, her voice more natural now. 'Oh, Peter, that's wonderful. Were you caddying?'

'That's just for scounging golf balls.'

Something happened in the room, some indefinable change in the air that registered against Peter's nerves. When he looked at Ken Fargo, the man was occupied in lighting a cigarette. Peter glanced at his mother but she was proudly smoothing out the bills and arranging them all face up before she put them in her handbag.

'Peter's been such a help,' she said to Fargo, an artificial heartiness in her soft voice. 'We've been just fine. I'm well enough to go back to work next week but it was very nice of you to drop by and see us.' She took two steps toward Fargo, her hand extended.

Fargo ignored the hand and sat down as if he meant to make a long visit. The knock at the door was a welcome diversion and Peter nearly collided with his mother as they both answered the summons.

'Oh, Mrs. Kiernan, have you seen my Victor?' It was Mrs. Anderson from across the street. Her three-year-old had such a perverse habit of straying that the distraught mother had taken to tying him to an old dog-run wire. 'I told Henry the rope was frayed. I was doing the wash out back and I just didn't notice. I suppose I should've checked when I didn't hear him fretting but I wanted to finish ... so I don't know how long he's been gone. Have you seen him? What with being home and all?'

Peter bristled but his mother shot him a look, reminding him that Mrs. Anderson was a nice woman and had more than a wayward Victor to burden her.

'No, Mrs. Anderson. I haven't seen Victor.'

'Which way is he likely to go, Mrs. Anderson?' asked Ken Fargo.

'Oh, I dunno. He could be halfway to town by now.' The woman twisted back the lock of lank bleached hair that had escaped her pins. She swiveled her body slightly, looking pointedly at the green Mustang at the curb.

'Well, that's no problem. C'mon, Pete, you and me will take a little spin and see if we can locate the lady's wandering boy.'

Peter gave his mother a swift look and she gave him a barely perceptible nod. A child was one of the lost items he could permissibly find.

'Shouldn't be no time at all before we have him safely back, Mrs. Anderson. Now don't worry. For one thing, I'm an insurance investigator and finding lost things is *my* business.'

Again that electric feeling charged the air, but before Peter could appeal to his mother, Kenny Fargo had hustled him out the door and into the car, all the time driveling reassurances to Mrs. Anderson.

'Roll down that window, Petey boy,' the man said and Peter set his teeth against the irritating familiarity. 'Keep a sharp eye out on your side. I'll take care of mine.'

Fargo's tone, smugly confident, gave Peter fair warning. Somehow Fargo knew that Peter could 'find' things. Somehow Peter must discourage him.

'You just sing out when you see that brat, Pete. This car'll stop on a dime and hand you back six cents . . . ha ha ha . . . inflation, you know.' Fargo deftly turned the Mustang into the road toward town. Peter let him although he knew that Victor Anderson was steadily moving in the opposite direction. 'And I got a bone to pick with you.'

Startled, Peter looked around but the man's frown was bogus.

'You should've let me know your mother was ill. She's a fine woman, your ma, and deserves the best. She could've had it if you'd let me know.'

'We got along all right.'

'Yeah, but she'd be well now with the proper food and care I could've provided. And I'd like to provide for her, you get what I mean?' An elbow prodded Peter in the ribs.

'We prefer to do things for ourselves.'

'You're a good kid, Peter, but there're things a man can do that a boy can't.'

Peter wanted to wipe that look from Fargo's face.

'Hey, you keep your eyes peeled for that kid. Let's find him in a hurry and get back. I got something to ask your ma and you might as well hear it.'

Peter obediently faced the window but they reached the middle of the town without a sight of any child.

'How about that? We gotta search the whole town? I thought you said the kid went into town.'

'No sir. Mrs. Anderson said she thought he'd be halfway to town by now.'

'Well, goddamit, where is he?'

Peter looked Ken Fargo straight in the eyes. 'I don't know.'

The man's face turned black and grim, then as suddenly assumed a forced good humor.

'All right, kid. If he didn't go into town, maybe he went out of town?'

'Maybe someone's found him already. There's Officer Scortius.'

The policeman was not the least bit pleased to hear that the Anderson kid was missing again and his remarks confirmed Peter's private opinion that Mrs. Anderson was a prime nuisance in the tiny community of Jennings, Colorado. Fargo brandished his investigator's credentials, an additional irritant to Scortius who'd been forced to muck around the countryside trying to find the lost shipment of furs 'alleged' to have been stashed somewhere near Jennings.

'Well, I'll see who we can find to help track the brat.'

'I'll do the main road out of town.'

Officer Scortius grunted and waddled off.

As they drew alongside her house, Mrs. Anderson was hanging over the gate, the picture of maternal anxiety. Clearly Victor had not been recovered but Fargo assured her heartily it was only a matter of moments and gunned the Mustang countryward.

'Okay, Peter, let's find that kid and end this soap opera,' Fargo said between his teeth. 'How far up the road is he?'

'Gee, how would I know?'

'How would you know? Because you'd know!'

The man's tone emphasized his certainty and Peter felt a sick fear curl up from the pit of his belly.

'I get around the country, Petey boy. And I hear things, interesting things.' He paused and his voice took on a conciliatory tone. 'Look, Petey boy, I like your mother. I want to take care of her the way a man can. She oughtn't to have to work herself sick to give you a decent place to live and a good education. I know how set she is to see you educated. But you don't need much book learning to get ahead. Not you. You know, with your trick, we could be a team, you and me. In fact, we could be a top-drawer unbeatable team of private investigators.'

That insistent, persuasive voice was bad enough: the arguments were worse. Fargo knew how to get to Peter.

'Wouldn't that be great? Your mother not having to work anymore? And you, kid, you've been handicapped. You've made mistakes. It was foolish, you know, to find Lyle Grauber's missing stocks! To say

nothing of that Cadillac in Colorado Springs!'
Fargo's laugh was unpleasant and Peter cringed.
That Cadillac business had meant they'd had to leave
one of the nicest apartments they'd had. That was
when they'd decided that Peter better check with
mother before he 'found' anything. There'd been a
fortune in that Cadillac . . . and he *couldn't* tell them
how he'd known where it was hidden. 'Yes,' Fargo
was saying in an ominously casual way, 'the police are
still looking for the kid who told them where to find
that Caddy – and skipped. They want him bad.'

The Mustang, like the Cadillac, had become a
trap.

'You must be mistaking me for someone else,
Mister Fargo,' Peter managed to say in a steady,
apologetic voice.

'Oh, no, I haven't. I'm a topflight investigator
because I'm smart. I put isolated clues together and
come up with open-and-shut convictions.'

If you looked adults in the face, they tended to
think you couldn't be lying: but it took every ounce
of self-control that Peter had learned in thirteen
years to look Ken Fargo squarely in the eyes.

'You got me wrong, Mister Fargo. What makes you
think I've ever been in Colorado Springs? And gee, if
I could find things, like you do, and get the reward,
I sure would for my mother's sake.'

'How do you know about rewards, kid?'

'Oh,' and Peter shrugged, 'you told mother once
that you get 10 per cent of the value of the stolen
items you recover for your company.'

Just the other side of the town limit sign, Fargo braked, swearing. Peter had 'located' Victor cutting across the Omers' meadow now, out of sight of the road. He knew he'd be obliged to find the child but he couldn't do so until he'd got rid of Ken Fargo, and how was he to do that?

'Where is the brat? C'mon, Peter. Where is he? You know!'

'No, Mister Fargo. I don't know.' And Peter stared the man directly in the eyes. 'I wish I did because Mrs. Anderson always tips 50 cents when someone brings Victor home.'

'You made seven bucks finding golf balls today. What about that?'

Peter forced himself to grin. 'All you have to do is watch where Mr. Roche slices his balls and then go bring 'em in when he isn't looking. Half the ones I brought in today were in the pond anyway.'

Doubt flickered across Ken Fargo's face.

'Honest, Mr. Fargo, I think you've got a case of mistaken identity.'

A big Olds came piling down the road toward town. Cursing under his breath, Fargo pushed himself out of the Mustang and flagged the big car down.

'Yeah, what's the trouble, fella? No gas?' asked the driver, sticking his head out the window. Peter saw, with sinking heart, that it was Mr. Roche and he tried to squinch down in the seat. 'Hi there, Pete. Find any more of my balls for me?' He flicked his cigarette to the roadside and gave Fargo his attention. 'Kid's a genius finding m'balls in the grass. Like he could home in on them or something. Caddy for me, Saturday, Pete? Ten sharp?'

Limp with defeat, Peter nodded and sank down in the bucket seat swallowing fiercely against the lump in his throat.

'Seen anything of a kid, too young to be off on his own?' asked Fargo.

'Kid? No. Nothing on the road from here to Hibernia.'

The Olds drove off, leaving Peter at Fargo's mercy.

' "Kid homes in on them or something, huh?" "No, Mr. Fargo, you got a case of mistaken identity!" ' Fargo's voice was savage as he slid into the driver's seat. 'All right, Peter me lad. Now unless you want some trouble, real trouble, with the cops in Colorado Springs – because they are looking for you – you better tell me where those furs are!'

'The furs?'

Fargo grabbed Peter by the wrist. He was as strong as he'd boasted and the bones in Peter's arm rubbed together painfully. Blunt fingers gouged into the tendons until Peter had all he could do not to cry out.

'You *know*, don't you?'

The surprise and pain had caught Peter off-guard. Fargo swore.

'How long have you known?' Each word was punctuated by a flexing of those implacable fingers in his arm. 'D'you realize you done me out of $15,000?' Just as Peter was certain Fargo was going to beat him, the man's attitude altered. 'Okay, kid. I understand. You and your mother got scared after that Cadillac caper. Well, you don't have to be scared anymore. I said we'd be a team and we will. No one will think it funny when *I* find things. I'm a first-rate investigator to begin with. But with you . . . okay, where's the furs?'

'In the old lead mine.' Peter pointed toward the hills.

'We already searched there.' Fargo's expression was suspicious. 'You lead me on, kid . . .' and he raised his hand menacingly.

'The furs are hidden under the rubble in the old ore carts.'

'How do you know? You seen 'em?'

'No, but that's where they are.'

'You mean we walked up and down past 'em?'

If they were mice they would've bit you, Peter thought, coining one of his mother's off-cited phrases. Thinking of his mother gave him a second hold on his courage.

'The road to the mine's around here, isn't it?'

Peter told Fargo the way.

'Now you're using the old noggin, Petey boy.' Cooperation made Fargo good-natured. 'Say kid, how do you do it?'

'What?'

'No more of the innocent act.' Fargo's voice took on a dangerous edge. 'How do you find things you've never seen?'

'I can't always,' Peter said, trying to sound dubious. 'It's just when things are on people's minds a lot, like that Cadillac or the furs, I sort of get a picture of where they are. Sometimes the picture is clearer than other times, and I know the location.'

'What's with the golf balls? You must've found hundreds of stupid golf balls these past couple'a months. Penny ante stuff – when I think of the lists of lost items on the company's records! I can make a fortune!'

Peter swallowed. 'I', not the more diplomatic 'we.' The Mustang swerved up the last bend to the mine. 'It's getting dark, Mister Fargo,' Peter said. 'We *could* come back tomorrow. We do have to find Victor . . . don't we?'

'Forget the brat, Pete. I've got a flashlight. We'll look in that mine now.' Fargo produced a huge handlight and motioned with it for Peter to lead the way.

'The mine's dangerous, Mister Fargo. And the ore carts are pretty far down . . .'

There was no reprieve in Fargo's eyes. Peter led the way.

The walls were dripping with the recent spring thaws and the tunnel had a clammy chill as they penetrated slowly down, turning the gentle bend that led into the bowels of the mine.

'That's a new fall,' Peter said nervously as they scrambled up over a soggy pile of mud.

Fargo shined the spot at the sagging supports. 'Yeah, so let's get this caper over with. $15,000 will do a lot for us, Petey boy. For you, your mother, and me.'

'Why don't you just take the furs and leave us alone, Mister Fargo? It's not right for me to find things for money.'

'Who says?' Fargo snorted at the altruism. 'Like the old saying, Petey, "losers weepers, finders keepers." And, Petey boy, I'm the finder's keeper from now on.'

The smile on Fargo's face chilled Peter worse than the tunnel's cold. But the smile disappeared when they both heard the groaning wood and the dribbling sound of dirt falling from a height.

'How much further? This place isn't safe.'

The ore carts were right up against the old fall which had closed the mine. Fargo hoisted Peter into the first cart. The boy dug into the loose earth layering the cart, and Fargo swore as Peter unearthed the first of the plastic sacks. 'They all that big? I can't picture packing these up that tunnel.' He heaved the plastic bags to the ground and the air puffed them up. 'I bet I can get the Mustang down the tunnel.' And he started off.

'Mister Fargo, would you leave the light here?' Peter cried.

Fargo turned, his smile malevolent in the dim light, for he kept the torch pointed forward. 'What? A big kid like you afraid of the dark?' He laughed. 'Just think of all the things $15,000 will buy.'

Peter watched with a rapidly increasing anxiety as

the gleam of the spot disappeared around the bend, leaving him in a total blackout.

'Afraid of the dark?' The taunt frightened him not half as much as the life looming with shadowy certitude before him. Not all the warmth of the pelts on which he crouched could have thawed the fear in Peter's heart.

An ominous creak, almost overhead, startled him further. 'The finder's keeper.' Fargo had said. There were darker death traps than an old mine shaft, and bleaker lightless vistas.

Nonetheless Peter cried aloud when he saw the return of light and heard the sound of the Mustang bumping along the cart tracks.

'Okay, move your butt and haul these furs into the car, Petey. On the double.'

Another warning rumble overhead and a gout of water from the support directly above the cars. Peter grabbed the plastic bags, tripping over the trailing length.

'Keep 'em off the wet ground, you stupid jerk. They're worth a fortune.'

Peter muttered an apology as he crammed them into the trunk. The plastic refused to give up its supply of air and Fargo was cursing as he helped. Then he stormed down the tunnel for more furs, dragging Peter with him. The light from the Mustang's headlights helped relieve the gloom, although its exhaust was a blue plume in the draughtless tunnel. Two loads and the trunk was full. Peter stood with an armload of plastic sacks wondering how they could possibly get them all in the sports car.

'Don't stand there, stupid. Dump 'em on the back seat.'

That too was full shortly, so Peter heaved his next load onto the passenger seat, falling over it as he lost his balance. Accidentally he hit the wheel, and the horn. The noise startled Fargo into dropping his load but his curses were covered by a long low rumble. Mud and ooze rained down.

Peter screamed, gesturing frantically to the bulging overhead beam. Then, suddenly, he found himself stumbling over plastic bags, desperately pulling at Fargo's arm to get the man to move. Peter remembered scrambling and clawing through wet heavy mud. Then something struck him across the head.

His skull was on fire, his body rigid. Frightened, certain he was buried in the tunnel, he tried to move but his arms were held to his side. His fingers clawed but met fluffy soft warm blanketting. There was noise and confusion around him. He was aware of breathing fresh air, and yet . . . there was thudding and rumbling underneath him which echoed through his pain-filled head.

The mine had collapsed! But he was wrapped in a blanket. He was safe!

'Yeah, you wouldn't believe how fast that Mustang went in reverse. The surprising thing is I made it out in one piece at all. 'Course the Company will see to the body work. All in the line of duty, Scortius! And I got what I went after. I found the furs.'

'I' found the furs? Peter cringed at Fargo's fatuous statement.

'You got real luck, Fargo,' Officer Scortius was saying enviously.

Fargo chuckled. 'Real luck! Say doc, how long does it take that ambulance to get here? I want Petey boy given the best of care. I'll take care of the bill myself.'

'The ambulance is coming,' said Dr. Wingard and there was something in his voice that made Peter think that the doctor didn't much like Ken Fargo. 'I'm just as anxious as you are about Peter's condition. I want an X-ray of that skull . . .'

'I thought you said that was just a flesh wound?'

'There's a possibility of concussion . . .'

'Concussion?' Fargo sounded startled.

'Yes, it was a wound caused by a falling object. And I want to run an ECG. I don't like the sound of that heart.'

'Heart?'

A fierce pounding in Peter's chest echoed the panic in Fargo's voice.

'Yes. Molly Kiernan's got enough on her mind, but I spotted an irregularity in Peter's heartbeat when I gave him a physical in school. Might be nothing. No mention of rheumatic fever on his school record . . .'

'Rheumatic fever?'

'I'm the cautious type. I'd just like to check.'

'Oh.'

Peter was somewhat encouraged by the dubious sound of Fargo's rejoinder. Then he remembered Jorie Favelly. She had a rheumatic heart and couldn't take gym and stayed out of school in hard weather and was a real twerp. Be like her? Peter groaned.

'Hey, he's coming to,' cried Fargo.

The air about Peter seemed to press in on him and he had a sense of suffocation. A hand grabbed his chin and shook him.

'Hey, Petey. Speak to me!'

There was a scuffle and an exclamation of surprise from Fargo.

'If you don't mind, Mr. Fargo, I'm the doctor.' A firm hand turned back the blanket and found Peter's wrist. 'And for your information, you don't shake the heads of concussion cases.' Boy, was Dr. Wingard angry! 'Peter? Peter? Can you hear me?' His voice was gentle again.

'Concussion.' That word again. A series of associations in Peter's mind got linked to TV shows he'd seen. Maybe . . . As his mother liked to say, there were more ways to kill a cat than choking him with butter.

'Where am I?' He fluttered his eyelids like patients did at Dr. Kildaire. The act became real for the daylight was bright enough to hurt his eyes.

'Peter, it's Dr. Wingard. How're you feeling?'

'My head hurts.'

'I know, boy. We'll soon fix that. Can you open your eyes again? And tell me how many fingers I'm holding up?'

Peter blinked. He could see that the doctor was holding up three fingers. He blinked again, made his eyes stay wide with fear.

'Who are you?' he asked, looking directly at the doctor as if he'd never seen him. Then he looked at Fargo. 'Where am I?'

'How many fingers, Peter?'

'Fingers? Fingers?' Peter couldn't think how many he ought to see if he didn't see the right number. But he could see the dawning of disappointed frustration and the fury of loss in Ken Fargo's face.

Losers weepers. Peter essayed a sob. After all, his head hurt – and he wasn't supposed to be as brave as Peter Kiernan.

'Who are you? Where am I? My head hurts.' But the first sob was abruptly followed by deep hurtful ones which Peter hadn't ordered.

'There there, boy. Take it easy. You'll be all right,' said the doctor. He stood up, pulling Fargo aside. Peter strained his ears. 'That head injury seems to be causing a little amnesia.'

'Amnesia?'

'Oh, I don't think it's anything to worry about. A few weeks' rest in the hospital, a careful regime for a few months and he'll be right as rain.'

'Amnesia? And a weak heart?' Fargo glanced sourly at Peter, who gave a weak groaning sob. 'Look, doc. I've got to report to my Company about finding those furs. You just send the bills for the kid to Midwestern!'

'You'll be looking in on Peter?'

Peter kept his eyes tightly shut, but he was thinking with all his strength: *Go away, Ken Fargo!*

Fargo cleared his throat and began moving away.

'Well now, I'll certainly try to. You let me know when he's completely recovered. If he gets his memory back. And check out that bad heart, too!'

Well, thought Peter, Petey boy just wouldn't recover ever from his amnesia. Not completely. And not that part of his mind that made him valuable to Fargo. *Finder's keeper, indeed!*

Weariness settled in along with pain and Peter closed his eyes. It was reassuring to hear little Victor blubbering. But what did he have to cry about? He was found, wasn't he?

Peter'd have to stop 'finding' anything for a while. Even Mr. Roche's golfballs. But he could blame that on the crack on the head, too. He could still caddy. Then when he grew up, and without Mr. Ken Fargo interfering with him and his mother, why *he'd* become the toppest flight insurance investigator. And nobody would find it odd that he could find anything he wanted.

As his mother often said, it was an ill wind that blew nobody any good.

*   *   *

ANNE McCAFFREY is one of today's most popular writers of fantasy fiction. Her *Pern* series, with its tales of dragons and a feudal society living on a long-lost Earth colony, started in 1968 with *Dragonflight* and has since won both the prestigious Hugo and Nebula awards. The success of these books has even inspired a study, *The Dragonlover's Guide to Pern* by Jody Lynn Nye (1989). A side-effect of this acclaim though, has been the overshadowing of her other important series, including the *Pegasus, Ireta, Killashandra* and *Planet Pirate* books which are all wonderful reads. This author of some sixty books, was born in America, but has lived in Ireland for many years. Her first fiction was published in the early 1950s in magazines of fantasy and science fiction, but following the success of the *Pern* books, her reputation has grown worldwide and in 2000 she was given a Lifetime Achievement Award by the British Fantasy Society. Two of Anne McCaffrey's books are of especial interest to younger readers: *The Girl Who Heard Dragons*, an anthology (1994) and *An Exchange of Gifts* (1995) in which a girl with a talent for growing things has to seek help from a young boy in order to live her own life. Like 'Finder Keepers', it is a remarkable story of a child with a unique gift.

THE BLACK DRESS

Alison Prince

Selina has bought an old black dress at a jumble sale. She just loves the soft silkiness of it, although her mother thinks it looks silly. Mum just can't understand why Selina would want to wear something so old-fashioned. Selina decides she has to find out what her best friend Christine thinks before she finally makes up her mind. So she puts on the dress and heads for her friend's home. On the way, though, a strange old man she has never seen before admires the dress and calls her by her name. Things get even scarier for Selina when she hears music coming from a ballroom which she knows has been closed for years and finds herself being drawn inside . . .

*　　*　　*

'Selina, *really*,' said Mrs Duncan. 'What *do* you look like?'

Selina picked up her handbag in silence. There was no point in arguing.

'Where *did* you get that ridiculous dress?' her mother persisted.

'At a jumble sale,' muttered Selina.

Mrs Duncan surveyed her daughter without enthusiasm. 'I can see it's got that nineteen thirtyish look,' she conceded. 'But you're much too young to wear that sort of thing, it's just silly. Where are you going, anyway?'

'Round to Christine's,' said Selina. 'I've finished my homework.'

Her mother sighed. 'Take a cardigan, then, for goodness' sake,' she said. 'The evenings are chilly now. And don't be too late back.'

Selina ran upstairs irritably. It was hardly worth going out at all if there had to be all this fuss. She stared at herself in the mirror. The square neck of the silky black dress was edged with embroidered flowers, pink and fawn on ivory-coloured net, and the skirt was double layered, with the under-skirt and the shorter top skirt both ending in deep bands of the same faded flowers. Selina's eyes stared anxiously back at her from under the dark fringe of her short-cropped hair. Did she really look silly? Yes, perhaps. She sat down on the edge of her bed, discouraged. The dress had seemed so lovely. She had found it on a hanger between a droopy ice-blue ball gown and a moth-eaten fur coat, and the minute she had touched its old, soft silkiness, she knew the dress had to be hers. She had borrowed two pounds from Christine to make up its cost, because the woman running the stall had said it was A Genuine.

'What are you doing?' her mother called up from the hall. 'If you're going out, just *go*.'

Christine had not seen the dress except on its hanger, Selina thought. If *she* thought it looked silly as well, then it would just have to be written off as a big mistake. She sighed, and put on a long, fawn, jumble-sale cardigan. Her mother didn't like that, either, but at least it covered up some of the offending dress. She picked up her bag and went downstairs.

'It's not that I always want to be at you,' her mother said in a kind of apology.

'I know,' said Selina. 'It's all right.' At the door, she looked back to add, 'I won't be late –' and caught the expression on her mother's face before it was quickly amended to a smile. Not so much annoyance, Selina thought, as an exasperated perplexity. And that was worse.

The pavements were still warm from the September sun and, beyond the roofs of the town, the sea sparkled, a fainter blue than the sky. After a few minutes, Selina found the cardigan too warm for comfort, so she took it off and slung it over her shoulder, then walked on self-consciously, eyeing passers-by for any signs of amusement at the old-fashioned dress. But the few people she passed seemed self-absorbed; parents with spade-trailing children, a couple of stout women in flowered dresses carrying macs and handbags, then a boy and girl with their arms round each other. Selina watched them covertly. The girl's thighs bulged in her over-tight jeans, and there was a groove across her back where her bra strap went. Why did he think she was attractive? Perhaps, Selina thought mournfully, it was because she wasn't ridiculous. She knew how to be what people expected.

Reaching Christine's house, Selina knocked on the

door. Mrs Dutton opened it and looked sympathetic. 'I'm afraid she's gone to play tennis, dear,' she said. 'Why don't you go and join them?' Then she glanced at the dress and added, 'Or were you planning to go somewhere special?'

'No,' said Selina. 'Nowhere at all. I'll see Christine another time.' Her voice was so determinedly cheerful that is sounded idiotic, and she retreated to the gate jauntily, treading on a clump of pinks with her high-heeled shoe as she wrestled with the latch. Somewhere special. So she *did* look silly. She waved airily at Mrs Dutton, who stared at her dubiously from the doorstep, and retraced her steps down the street.

Now what? Selina tried to feel brisk and purposeful as she walked on, though in fact the bottom had dropped out of her evening. It was unthinkable to return home so soon. She could almost hear her mother's voice; 'Oh, dear. And after you got all dressed up, too.'

The steeply-sloping roads of the little town issued a natural invitation to follow them down towards the sea. Feeling as conspicuous as a Christmas tree, Selina walked past the sun-warmed garden walls and fuchsia hedges until the houses gave way to small hotels and the road eventually ended at the High Street. The shops were closed, but at least Selina could pretend to be interested in the goods displayed in their windows, which felt better than aimless walking. Then she stopped.

A group of boys lounged round the bus shelter outside the Plaza cinema. Neil Coppard and his friends. Selina prickled with dread. Of all the noisy, self-confident boys at school, Neil frightened her the most. 'Hello, Sleena,' he would say, with a mocking grin. She could not walk past him, not in this dress. She dived down an alleyway beside Alexander's, who sold postcards and beach balls, and emerged on to the promenade, where she crossed over to walk beside the ornate railings, running her hand casually along their rust-streaked white paint. It was better here. In a hundred yards or so she would be at the pier, which seemed like a proper objective. Not that the pier was anything wonderful. It boasted a string of coloured lights over its entrance, but consisted of nothing more than a long stretch of decking, punctuated by occasional wrought-iron benches. At the pier's far end was the long-disused ballroom, with its windows boarded up and planks of wood nailed across its entrance. Its peeling walls were richly adorned with graffiti and there were frequent letters in the local paper calling on the Council to do something about it.

The sun's lower edge was just touching the horizon and the path of pinkish light it cast across the water was ruffled suddenly by a sharp evening breeze. As she walked along the pier, Selina started to put her cardigan on but, with the clumsiness that caused her so much despair, she lost control of her handbag, which slipped from under her arm to fall on the wooden planks, almost at the feet of an old man sitting on a seat. He picked the bag up and held it out to her with a smile.

'Thank you,' she said in confusion.

The old man seemed unperturbed. 'Quite a chilly breeze,' he remarked. He watched Selina as she finished struggling into the cardigan, then said, 'What a very charming dress.'

He seemed absolutely sincere. Selina smiled at him. 'I think it's nice, too,' she said. 'But I wasn't sure. I mean, it *is* awfully old-fashioned.'

The old man did not seem to be listening, although his blue eyes continued to survey Selina from under the brim of a hat which reminded her of a Humphrey Bogart film. He wore his coat collar turned up in a Bogartish way, too, but his face was thin and he seemed a shrunken remnant of what he must once have been. 'It reminds me,' he said, still staring at the black dress, 'reminds me . . . Selina wore a dress like that.' His gaze drifted away.

'But that's my name!' said Selina, startled. Perhaps the old man was someone she ought to recognise. 'Are you a friend of my mother's?' she asked. 'She works at the library, she knows lots of people.'

The old man seemed not to hear. Selina stood and looked at him, wishing he would speak to her again. With a sudden, unreasoning intensity, she wanted to know how he knew her name, and what the memories were that the black dress had stirred in him. He gave a little sigh, but his eyes gazed at something Selina could not see, and his smile was not caused by anything she could understand.

Then she heard music, borne very faintly on the wind.

'Perhaps it's buskers!' she said. She liked the impromptu performances by the hairy-socks-wearing people from the Youth Hostel – but as the music became more distinct, she realised that it was not the kind of sound that buskers made. It was a dance band, playing with the tired, professional sweetness of many long, repetitive nights. 'No,' she said, still hoping to stir the old man into further conversation. 'It's just someone with a transistor.'

The old man extended a bony, papery hand courteously, but not to Selina. 'Allow me,' he said to some unseen person.

Wandering in his mind, Selina thought. Old people often got like that – and yet it was oddly disappointing not to be able to follow him into whatever world it was that he saw. Alone again, she turned away and walked on towards the disused ballroom. The Council seemed to have cleaned it up a bit, she noticed. The graffiti had gone, and its paint looked a lot fresher. Attracted by the music, she walked along the narrow strip of the pier beside the ballroom until she reached the open space behind it, where anglers sat on summer afternoons with their Thermos flasks and extra sweaters and horrible tins of bait. There was nobody here now, with or without a transistor and yet the music played on. Selina walked back along the other side of the ballroom, still hunting for the source of the elusive music, but she seemed to be the only person on the pier apart from the old man who still sat on his seat in the last rays of the sun.

Suddenly the music seemed much louder. Selina swung round. Of course! It was coming from inside the ballroom. And, for the first time, she saw that the windows were no longer boarded up. Their blank appearance was due to long curtains hanging inside the glass, and cracks of light gleamed from within them. So the Council really were doing something with the place at last! How stupid not to have noticed it before – she had been so intent on the music. Selina ran towards the ballroom's entrance and found that there, too, the nailed-up planks of wood had gone. She pushed at one of the long doors, which opened at her touch.

Inside, Selina gasped. The Council had done a good job. The entrance hall had been completely restored to its former glory, with lights twinkling over the gilt-framed mirrors and heavy velvet curtains draped across the entrance to the dance floor. There was a thick, heady smell of perfume and dusty carpets.

Selina made her way to the pay-desk, where a woman in a tight black dress and a lot of make-up was filing her nails.

'Excuse me,' Selina said, 'but can you tell me what's going on? I mean, is it going to be a Theatre Centre or a club, or what?'

The woman gazed at her uncomprehendingly.

'Allow me,' said a voice from behind Selina. 'May I escort you?'

'Oh, but I couldn't –' Selina began. She looked up at the young man who had spoken, and he smiled.

'Of course you couldn't,' he agreed. 'A well-brought-up girl like you wouldn't dream of it.' He wore a pale grey suit, pin-striped in white, and a long, puckered scar ran from his fair hair down the left-hand side of his forehead, bisecting his eyebrow and ending just above his eye. He saw her looking at it. 'If you would rather not partner someone who looks like Frankenstein,' he said, 'I will quite understand.'

Selina looked into his blue eyes and found herself saying, 'I'd like to very much. Thank you.' She heard her own words in astonishment. Less than half an hour ago, she had crossed the road and fled down an alleyway for fear of even being *seen* by Neil Coppard and his friends, and yet here she was, accepting the company of a total stranger. Was she dreaming? She laughed a little breathlessly.

'Thank you,' said the young man gravely. 'If you would like to leave your wrap, I'll wait for you here.'

In the Ladies' Powder Room, Selina found another black-clad woman behind a counter, and handed in the fawn cardigan. Girls stood at the mirrors, patting at their hair and applying more make-up, and Selina almost laughed aloud at their appearance. All of them wore dresses similar to her own, retrieved, she supposed, from secondhand shops and jumble sales, though they looked in remarkably good condition. Several of the girls wore bandeaux round their crimped hair, some with feathers in them, and bangles were much in evidence, often worn above the elbow. Selina opened her bag and took out a comb, and a pale pink lipstick which was her only item of make-up. Her mother didn't approve of cosmetics.

The girl next to Selina finished applying mascara to her already darkened eyelashes and screwed the brush back into the little bottle, then caught Selina's glance of envy. 'Want to borrow it, love?' she offered.

'Could I really?' asked Selina. She would have to sneak up to the bathroom as soon as she got home, to wash it off before her mother saw it.

'Yes, go on,' said the girl. 'I know what it is when you first leave school. Got no money for anything, have you? Tell you what – you want me to make you look really nice?' Not waiting for an answer, she pointed to a gilt chair and added, 'Sit down there.'

'I didn't know they were doing anything with this place,' Selina began as she sat down obediently.

'Shut your eyes,' her new friend instructed. 'And don't chatter – it puts me off.' After some busy minutes with eyeshadow and mascara and powder, she added, 'There. How's that look?'

Selina stared at herself in the mirror. The face which stared back seemed to belong to somebody else – an older, more sophisticated girl, whose dark-rimmed eyes and palely powdered skin made the black dress for the first time seem utterly suited to its owner. She turned to the girl and smiled. 'Thank you,' she said.

The girl smiled back, ramming things into her silk bag. 'You'll knock your partner cold,' she said.

When Selina went back into the foyer, the young man did, in fact, seem impressed. He raised her hand to his lips and kissed it, and his blue eyes stared into hers with a pleasure and gratitude which made her feel almost sad. 'I am truly privileged,' he said. Then he held the velvet curtain aside, and she went before him into the ballroom.

Here, too, everything had been perfectly restored. Potted palms stood on the platform beside the band and small gilt chairs and tables surrounded the dance floor. Selina remembered with gratitude how Miss Barnet, the PE mistress at school, had insisted on teaching them ballroom dancing when the field was too wet for hockey in the winter term. Everyone had grumbled like mad about it, but Miss Barnet had insisted that it was something which always came in handy. Too true!

'My name is Bertie Pomfret,' said the young man as he led Selina into a slow foxtrot. 'Awfully silly, I'm afraid.'

'You don't have to keep apologising,' said Selina. 'My name's a bit silly, too – Selina. I get laughed at.'

'It's a beautiful name,' said Bertie. 'And it suits you perfectly.'

It was the best evening of Selina's life. For once, she felt assured instead of clumsy, and nothing seemed to matter except the awareness of the music and of Bertie's hand firmly on her back as they danced. Her curiosity about the transformation of the disused ballroom to this palace of joy seemed irrelevant, specially as nobody else showed the slightest concern about it. Obviously, she thought, the place must have been converted some time ago and these dances were regular features. She did not often come down to the pier in the summer when the town was full of tourists.

Emboldened as they sat over glasses of lemonade at one of the little gilt tables, she looked at the scar which ran down Bertie's forehead, the legacy of such a terrible wound, and asked, 'How did you get that?'

'A German bayonet,' he said, and smiled wryly. 'The closest shave I ever had.'

Selina did not understand what he meant, but as she tried to frame another question, the lights dimmed and the band struck up a slow waltz. The faceted mirror ball in the centre of the ceiling began to revolve as Bertie stood up and offered her his hand, casting a shifting array of brilliant flickers across walls and floor, over the dancers and the band and the potted palms, over white arms, nodding feathers and the stately heads of the rotating couples.

'The last waltz,' Bertie said in her ear, 'of a perfect evening.'

As she danced, Selina felt that the whirling flecks of light made her weightless, as if she and the fair-haired young man moved in a galaxy of stars where nothing was still, and the only certainty was the ceaseless movement of their circling.

As the music ended, Bertie turned his face to Selina's and, very gently, kissed her. The lights came up and the band played the first half of the National Anthem at a brisk, impatient pace while the dancers stood immobile. Then it was over.

Bertie said, 'Thank you. I shall remember this evening as long as I live.'

'So shall I,' said Selina with conviction as they made their way off the floor with the other dancers. 'It's been wonderful.'

In the foyer, they paused. 'May I see you home?' Bertie asked. 'Where do you live?'

'Up in Albany Terrace,' said Selina. 'Yes, that would be lovely.' To be seen in the company of this young man would be the last drop in her cup of happiness. She didn't mind his scarred face. He was wonderful. She hoped Neil Coppard and his friends were still hanging about as she and Bertie walked up the High Street. She would never be scared of Neil again. She was a different person now. 'I'll just get my cardigan,' she added.

'I shall be outside,' said Bertie.

In the cloakroom, Selina stared at her still-unfamiliar dark-eyed face in the mirror. In the black dress, she looked almost beautiful.

'Did you have a nice time?' asked the girl who had made her up.

'*Brilliant*,' said Selina.

Outside, strangely, it was still light. Selina frowned in the unexpected rays of the setting sun. Surely it should be pitch dark by now?

There was nobody about. A little distance away, the old man still sat on his bench, leaning slightly sideways now. His hat, Selina saw, had fallen off and lay on the wooden decking beside him. He must have gone to sleep. She turned impatiently to the ballroom's entrance, expecting to see the grey-suited figure of Bertie Pomfret coming to meet her – and her heart gave a wild leap of shock.

The ballroom was as derelict and abandoned as ever. Planks of wood were nailed across its door and the windows were boarded up. Its peeling grey stucco was once more grotesquely adorned with close-packed graffiti, ranging from huge statements in coloured spray-can to detailed obscenities scrawled with pencils and lipsticks and felt-tip pens.

Selina felt dizzy and slightly sick. Something had happened to her which her mind was unable to encompass. Had she slept as she stood here, and dreamed the whole thing in a long, hallucinated instant? The shock was followed by an overwhelming sense of grief as she realised that it was no use waiting for Bertie Pomfret. The gentle young man with the scarred face did not exist. She would not walk home through the town at his side. There would be no showing-off her new, triumphant status to Neil Coppard or anyone else. And, to make things worse, she saw Neil himself at the end of the pier, approaching with his gaggle of friends.

For a moment, her old panic assailed her. Then she knew that she was not afraid of Neil Coppard. She would simply let him walk past, in a perfectly civilised way. She set off along the pier towards the boys, but paused as she passed the old man on the bench. He had retrieved her bag for her, so she could at least retrieve his hat.

The old man had slumped a little further sideways, and as Selina bent down to pick up the hat, her face came level with his. The blue eyes were open, but they stared at nothing. He was not a person any more. He had become a thing.

And then she saw the scar.

It ran from the old man's white hair down the left side of his forehead, bisecting the eyebrow to end just above the open, unmoving eyes. Selina crammed her hand over her mouth, trying to stop the great gulping sobs, but it was no good. Reality had done a terrible somersault and left her standing here, staring at a dead man who had kissed her a few minutes ago, in a time which had been true then, but mocked her now with its impossibility.

'Sleena,' said Neil Coppard, coming up to her. 'What's the matter?'

Still clutching the old man's hat, Selina shook her head blindly. She could not tear her eyes from the long, puckered scar on the dead face.

The boys bent over the old man, and one of them gave a low whistle of concern. 'Snuffed it,' said another. They looked at each other in embarrassment, uncertain what to do.

'You lot, go and find the fuzz,' said Neil. 'Ring 999 or something. I'll stay here.'

The boys set off at a run.

Surprisingly gently, Neil took the old man's hat from Selina and laid it on the bench beside its owner. Then he put his hand under Selina's elbow and led her to an empty bench. 'Sit down,' he said.

This was crazier than ever, Selina thought in the midst of the confusion which raged in her mind. Neil Coppard, here beside her instead of Bertie. Fighting for self-control, she groped in her handbag for a tissue and managed to say, 'Sorry to be so silly.'

'It's all right,' said Neil. 'Tell you, I feel a bit shaky too, seeing the old boy sitting there like that. I was talking to him only yesterday.'

'Were you?' Selina looked up sharply, oblivious of her tear-blotched face. 'Who is he?' she asked. 'What's his name?' But she knew what the answer would be.

'Mr Pomfret,' said Neil. 'He used to live next door to us before he went into the Old People's Home. He was ever so ancient. Must have been about ninety.'

'Was he married?' Selina persisted, and again answered the question in her own mind. Yes, to a girl called Selina.

'He used to be,' said Neil. 'She died years ago – before I was born, I think, or around then.'

'He met her here,' said Selina, needing to tell someone what had happened. 'He was remembering it.'

'Might have done,' Neil agreed. 'We'll never know, will we?'

Selina shook her head. Tears threatened again. Neil watched her, and even in the middle of her distress, she found that she was noticing his bare arms and his faded pink sleeveless T-shirt, paler than his brown skin. Why wasn't he cold? She herself had begun to shiver. After a few minutes, Neil said, 'I like that dress.'

Selina gave a laugh that was half a sob. Bertie had liked it, too.

'What's funny?' asked Neil.

It was too difficult to explain. 'My mother said I looked ridiculous,' Selina said.

''Spect she's jealous,' said Neil.

The boys came back with a policeman, and there were endless questions. Selina told him she had walked round the ballroom and looked at the sea for a while, and when she came back, she had seen that the old man was dead.

'How long were you looking at the sea?' asked the policeman, pencil poised.

Selina stared out across the colourless water. 'I don't know,' she said. 'It could have been just a moment, or it could have been hours.'

Walking up the High Street with Neil beside her, Selina continued to wrestle with the puzzle of what had happened to her. If the ballroom had only existed in some kind of long hallucination, how had she been so sure of old Mr Pomfret's name? Or had he mentioned it during their brief conversation when he had picked up her bag? She could not be sure. No, she decided with regret, things like that simply did not happen. It had all taken place in a waking dream. There was only one reality. She stared

at the cracks in the pavement as she walked, and saw
Neil's dilapidated trainers as he paced beside her.
One day, she thought, she might tell him all about
what had happened. When she knew him better.

Neil said, 'You're very quiet.'

'So are you,' said Selina defensively.

Neil shrugged. 'I didn't want to interrupt,' he said.
'You seemed to be miles away.'

They arrived at her gate. 'This is my house,' said
Selina, and turned to look at him, conscience-
stricken. He had walked all this way with her, and she
had hardly spoken a word to him, and yet she was
taking it for granted that she would one day know
him better. What an idiot!

'I'm sorry,' she said. 'You'll think I'm awfully rude.
And you've been so –' She could not find a word
which did not upset her. So gentle. So kind. With
them came a vision of the fair-haired boy with the
scarred face. 'So great,' she blurted, and embarrass-
ingly, her eyes swam with tears again.

'Couldn't let you come home on your own, could
I?' said Neil. 'You might have passed out or something. I mean, it's a hell of a shock.' Then he looked
at her and grinned. 'You haven't half made your eyes
run,' he said. 'You look as if you've been down a coal
mine.'

Selina laughed, and dabbed at her eyes with the
tissue she still held crumpled in her hand. Then she
gasped as she realised what he had said. The tissue,
she saw, was black-streaked with mascara. 'So it *did*
happen!' she exclaimed.

'What did?' asked Neil.

She shook her head. It was too complicated. 'You'll think I'm mad,' she said.

'Sane people are boring,' said Neil cheerfully. 'Look, tell me about it tomorrow, okay? It's getting too cold to hang about here. I'll see you after school. We'll go down the caff.'

'Okay,' said Selina, and nodded several times in promise and agreement. 'Yes. And thanks for everything.'

'Any time,' said Neil.

Selina stood at the gate and watched him as he ran away down the street, turning once to wave. She waved back. Then she opened the gate and walked up the path to the house, taking her key out of her bag. She would go straight upstairs, to take off the black dress and wash her face. There would be an awful row if her mother caught her wearing make-up.

*   *   *

ALISON PRINCE is an accomplished artist as well as a poet and writer of stories for younger readers. She began drawing as a child and at the age of thirteen won a BBC *Children's Hour* play-writing competition. Later she worked on the *Trumpton* TV series and was responsible for the immortal line, 'Pugh, Pugh, Barney McGrew, Cuthbert, Dibble and Grub'. Her reputation was ensured with the contemporary Glaswegian Robin Hood story, *The Sherwood Hero*, which won The *Guardian* Children's Fiction Award in 1996.

Born in Kent, Alison Prince spent 'some acutely boring years at a girl's grammar school, before winning a scholarship to the Slade School of Art. One of her early jobs was as a trainee telegraphist at Cable & Wireless where she taught herself to type by writing a ghost story. When this was printed out on a machine in the mahogany-panelled office upstairs, she was promptly sacked! However, despite other jobs in teaching and running a farm, she never lost her fascination with the supernatural and subsequently used it as the theme of several of her most popular children's titles, including *The Ghost Within* (1984), *Haunted Children* (1986) and the collection of stories in which music intermingles with the mysterious: *A Haunting Refrain* (1988).

THE SUSSEX VAMPIRE

Arthur Conan Doyle

Jack is fifteen. He's a lonely and rather sensitive boy. His mother died some years ago and now his father has remarried. Jack's step-mother has just had a baby boy and, for his dad's sake, the lad is trying to get on with both of them. Then a series of frightening events happen in the baby's room. The infant is found with a small wound on his neck and blood dribbling on to the sheets. On another night of horror, the baby's nurse discovers the mother leaning over her child with blood all round her lips. Is it a case of vampirism? There is only one man to solve this mystery – the great detective, Sherlock Holmes, and his assistant, Doctor Watson – and Jack finds himself caught up in one of the scariest cases ever tackled by the famous sleuth of Baker Street.

*   *   *

HOLMES had read carefully a note which the last post had brought him. Then, with the dry chuckle which was his nearest approach to a laugh, he tossed it over to me.

'For a mixture of the modern and the mediæval, of the practical and of the wildly fanciful, I think this is surely the limit,' said he. 'What do you make of it, Watson?'

I read as follows:

46 OLD JEWRY,
Nov. 19th.

Re Vampires.

SIR,—

Our client, Mr. Robert Ferguson, of Ferguson &
Muirhead, tea brokers, of Mincing Lane, has made
some inquiry from us in a communication of even
date concerning vampires. As our firm specializes
entirely upon the assessment of machinery the
matter hardly comes within our purview, and we
have therefore recommended Mr. Ferguson to call
upon you and lay the matter before you. We have
not forgotten your successful action in the case of
Matilda Briggs.

We are, Sir, faithfully yours,
MORRISON, MORRISON, AND DODD.
per E. J. C.

'Matilda Briggs was not the name of a young
woman, Watson,' said Holmes, in a reminiscent
voice. 'It was a ship which is associated with the giant
rat of Sumatra, a story for which the world is not yet
prepared. But what do we know about vampires?
Does it come within our purview either? Anything is
better than stagnation, but really we seem to have
been switched on to a Grimm's fairy tale. Make a
long arm, Watson, and see what V has to say.'

I leaned back and took down the great index
volume to which he referred. Holmes balanced it on
his knee and his eyes moved slowly and lovingly over

the record of old cases, mixed with the accumulated information of a lifetime.

'Voyage of the *Gloria Scott*,' he read. 'That was a bad business. I have some recollection that you made a record of it, Watson, though I was unable to congratulate you upon the result. Victor Lynch, the forger. Venomous lizard or gila. Remarkable case, that! Vittoria, the circus belle. Vanderbilt and the Yeggman. Vipers. Vigor, the Hammersmith wonder. Hullo! Hullo! Good old index. You can't beat it. Listen to this, Watson. Vampirism in Hungary. And again, Vampires in Transylvania.' He turned over the pages with eagerness, but after a short, intent perusal he threw down the great book with a snarl of disappointment.

'Rubbish, Watson, rubbish! What have we to do with walking corpses who can only be held in their grave by stakes driven through their hearts? It's pure lunacy.'

'But surely,' said I, 'the vampire was not necessarily a dead man? A living person might have the habit. I have read, for example, of the old sucking the blood of the young in order to retain their youth.'

'You are right, Watson. It mentions the legend in one of these references. But are we to give serious attention to such things? This Agency stands flat-footed upon the ground, and there it must remain. The world is big enough for us. No ghosts need apply. I fear that we cannot take Mr. Robert Ferguson very seriously. Possibly this note may be from him, and may throw some light upon what is worrying him.'

He took up a second letter which had lain unnoticed upon the table whilst he had been absorbed with the first. This he began to read with a smile of amusement upon his face which gradually faded away into an expression of intense interest and concentration. When he had finished he sat for some little time lost in thought with the letter dangling from his fingers. Finally, with a start, he aroused himself from his reverie.

'Cheeseman's, Lamberley. Where is Lamberley, Watson?'

'It is in Sussex, south of Horsham.'

'Not very far, eh? And Cheeseman's?'

'I know that country, Holmes. It is full of old houses which are named after the men who built them centuries ago. You get Odley's and Harvey's and Carriton's – the folk are forgotten but their names live in their houses.'

'Precisely,' said Holmes coldly. It was one of the peculiarities of his proud, self-contained nature that, though he docketed any fresh information very quickly and accurately in his brain, he seldom made any acknowledgment to the giver. 'I rather fancy we shall know a good deal more about Cheeseman's, Lamberley, before we are through. The letter is, as I had hoped, from Robert Ferguson. By the way, he claims acquaintance with you.'

'With me!'

'You had better read it.'

He handed the letter across. It was headed with the address quoted.

DEAR MR. HOLMES, (it said) – I have been recommended to you by my lawyers, but indeed the matter is so extraordinarily delicate that it is most difficult to discuss. It concerns a friend for whom I am acting. This gentleman married some five years ago a Peruvian lady, the daughter of a Peruvian merchant, whom he had met in connection with the importation of nitrates. The lady was very beautiful, but the fact of her foreign birth and of her alien religion always caused a separation of interests and of feelings between husband and wife, so that after a time his love may have cooled towards her and he may have come to regard their union as a mistake. He felt there were sides of her character which he could never explore or understand. This was the more painful as she was as loving a wife as a man could have – to all appearance absolutely devoted.

Now for the point which I will make more plain when we meet. Indeed, this note is merely to give you a general idea of the situation and to ascertain whether you would care to interest yourself in the matter. The lady began to show some curious traits, quite alien to her ordinarily sweet and gentle disposition. The gentleman had been married twice and he had one son by the first wife. This boy was now fifteen, a very charming and affectionate youth, though unhappily injured through an accident in childhood. Twice the wife was caught in the act of assaulting this poor lad in the most unprovoked way. Once she struck him with a stick and left a great weal on his arm.

This was a small matter, however, compared with her conduct to her own child, a dear boy just under one year of age. On one occasion about a month ago this child had been left by its nurse for a few minutes. A loud cry from the baby, as of pain, called the nurse back. As she ran into the room she saw her employer, the lady, leaning over the baby and apparently biting his neck. There was a small wound in the neck, from which a stream of blood had escaped. The nurse was so horrified that she wished to call the husband, but the lady implored her not to do so, and actually gave her five pounds as a price for her silence. No explanation was ever given, and for the moment the matter was passed over.

It left, however, a terrible impression upon the nurse's mind, and from that time she began to watch her mistress closely, and to keep a closer guard upon the baby, whom she tenderly loved. It seemed to her that even as she watched the mother, so the mother watched her, and that every time she was compelled to leave the baby alone the mother was waiting to get at it. Day and night the nurse covered the child, and day and night the silent, watchful mother seemed to be lying in wait as a wolf waits for a lamb. It must read most incredible to you, and yet I beg you to take it seriously, for a child's life and a man's sanity may depend upon it.

At last there came one dreadful day when the facts could no longer be concealed from the husband. The nurse's nerve had given way; she could stand the strain no longer, and she made a clean breast of it all to the man. To him it seemed as wild a tale as it may now seem to you. He knew his wife to be a loving wife, and, save for the assaults upon her stepson, a loving mother. Why, then, should she wound her own dear little baby? He told the nurse that she was dreaming, that her suspicions were those of a lunatic, and that such libels upon her mistress were not to be tolerated. Whilst they were talking, a sudden cry of pain was heard. Nurse and master rushed together to the nursery. Imagine his feelings, Mr. Holmes, as he saw his wife rise from a kneeling position beside the cot, and saw blood upon the child's exposed neck and upon the sheet. With a cry of horror, he turned his wife's face to the light and saw blood all round her lips. It was she – she beyond all question – who had drunk the poor baby's blood.

So the matter stands. She is now confined to her room. There has been no explanation. The husband is half demented. He knows, and I know, little of Vampirism beyond the name. We had thought it was some wild tale of foreign parts. And yet here in the very heart of the English Sussex – well, all this can be discussed with you in the morning. Will you see me? Will you use your great powers in aiding a distracted man? If so, kindly wire to Ferguson, Cheeseman's, Lamberley, and I will be at your rooms by ten o'clock.

Yours faithfully,
ROBERT FERGUSON.

PS. – I believe your friend Watson played Rugby for Blackheath when I was three-quarter for Richmond. It is the only personal introduction which I can give.

'Of course I remember him,' said I, as I laid down the letter. 'Big Bob Ferguson, the finest three-quarter Richmond ever had. He was always a good-natured chap. It's like him to be so concerned over a friend's case.'

Holmes looked at me thoughtfully and shook his head. 'I never get your limits, Watson,' said he. 'There are unexplored possibilities about you. Take a wire down, like a good fellow. "Will examine your case with pleasure."'

'*Your* case!'

'We must not let him think that this Agency is a home for the weak-minded. Of course it is his case. Send him that wire and let the matter rest till morning.'

Promptly at ten o'clock next morning Ferguson strode into our room. I had remembered him as a long, slab-sided man with loose limbs and a fine turn of speed, which had carried him round many an opposing back. There is surely nothing in life more painful than to meet the wreck of a fine athlete whom one has known in his prime. His great frame had fallen in, his flaxen hair was scanty, and his shoulders were bowed. I fear that I roused corresponding emotions in him.

'Hullo, Watson,' said he, and his voice was still deep and hearty. 'You don't look quite the man you did when I threw you over the ropes into the crowd at the Old Deer Park. I expect I have changed a bit also. But it's this last day or two that has aged me. I see by your telegram, Mr. Holmes, that it is no use my pretending to be anyone's deputy.'

'It is simpler to deal direct,' said Holmes.

'Of course it is. But you can imagine how difficult it is when you are speaking of the one woman whom you are bound to protect and help. What can I do? How am I to go to the police with such a story? And yet the kiddies have got to be protected. Is it madness, Mr. Holmes? Is it something in the blood? Have you any similar case in your experience? For God's sake, give me some advice, for I am at my wits' end.'

'Very naturally, Mr. Ferguson. Now sit here and pull yourself together and give me a few clear answers. I can assure you that I am very far from being at my wits' end, and that I am confident we shall find some solution. First of all, tell me what steps you have taken. Is your wife still near the children?'

'We had a dreadful scene. She is a most loving woman, Mr. Holmes. If ever a woman loved a man with all her heart and soul, she loves me. She was cut to the heart that I should have discovered this horrible, this incredible, secret. She would not even speak. She gave no answer to my reproaches, save to gaze at me with a sort of wild, despairing look in her eyes. Then she rushed to her room and locked herself in. Since then she has refused to see me. She has a maid who was with her before her marriage, Dolores by name – a friend rather than a servant. She takes her food to her.'

'Then the child is in no immediate danger?'

'Mrs. Mason, the nurse, has sworn that she will not leave it night or day. I can absolutely trust her. I am more uneasy about poor little Jack, for, as I told you in my note, he has twice been assaulted by her.'

'But never wounded?'

'No; she struck him savagely. It is the more terrible as he is a poor little inoffensive cripple.' Ferguson's gaunt features softened as he spoke of his boy. 'You would think that the dear lad's condition would soften anyone's heart. A fall in childhood and a twisted spine, Mr. Holmes. But the dearest, most loving heart within.'

Holmes had picked up the letter of yesterday and was reading it over. 'What other inmates are there in your house, Mr. Ferguson?'

'Two servants who have not been long with us. One stable-hand, Michael, who sleeps in the house. My wife, myself, my boy Jack, baby, Dolores, and Mrs. Mason. That is all.'

'I gather that you did not know your wife well at the time of your marriage?'

'I had only known her a few weeks.'

'How long had this maid Dolores been with her?'

'Some years.'

'Then your wife's character would really be better known by Dolores than by you?'

'Yes, you may say so.'

Holmes made a note.

'I fancy,' said he, 'that I may be of more use at Lamberley than here. It is eminently a case for personal investigation. If the lady remains in her room, our presence could not annoy or inconvenience her. Of course, we would stay at the inn.'

Ferguson gave a gesture of relief.

'It is what I hoped, Mr. Holmes. There is an excellent train at two from Victoria, if you could come.'

'Of course we could come. There is a lull at present. I can give you my undivided energies. Watson, of course, comes with us. But there are one or two points upon which I wish to be very sure before I start. This unhappy lady, as I understand it, has appeared to assault both the children, her own baby and your little son?'

'That is so.'

'But the assaults take different forms, do they not? She has beaten your son.'

'Once with a stick and once very savagely with her hands.'

'Did she give no explanation why she struck him?'

'None, save that she hated him. Again and again she said so.'

'Well, that is not unknown among stepmothers. A posthumous jealousy, we will say. Is the lady jealous by nature?'

'Yes, she is very jealous – jealous with all the strength of her fiery tropical love.'

'But the boy – he is fifteen, I understand, and probably very developed in mind, since his body has been circumscribed in action. Did he give you no explanation of these assaults?'

'No; he declared there was no reason.'

'Were they good friends at other times?'

'No; there was never any love between them.'

'Yet you say he is affectionate?'

'Never in the world could there be so devoted a son. My life is his life. He is absorbed in what I say or do.'

Once again Holmes made a note. For some time he sat lost in thought.

'No doubt you and the boy were great comrades before this second marriage. You were thrown very close together, were you not?'

'Very much so.'

'And the boy, having so affectionate a nature, was devoted, no doubt, to the memory of his mother?'

'Most devoted.'

'He would certainly seem to be a most interesting lad. There is one other point about these assaults. Were the strange attacks upon the baby and the assaults upon your son at the same period?'

'In the first case it was so. It was as if some frenzy had seized her, and she had vented her rage upon both. In the second case it was only Jack who suffered. Mrs. Mason had no complaint to make about the baby.'

'That certainly complicates matters.'

'I don't quite follow you, Mr. Holmes.'

'Possibly not. One forms provisional theories and waits for time or fuller knowledge to explode them. A bad habit, Mr. Ferguson; but human nature is weak. I fear that your old friend here has given an exaggerated view of my scientific methods. However, I will only say at the present stage that your problem does not appear to me to be insoluble, and that you may expect to find us at Victoria at two o'clock.'

It was evening of a dull, foggy November day when, having left our bags at the 'Chequers,' Lamberley, we drove through the Sussex clay of a long winding lane, and finally reached the isolated and ancient farmhouse in which Ferguson dwelt. It was a large, straggling building, very old in the centre, very new at the wings, with towering Tudor chimneys and a lichen-spotted, high-pitched roof of Horsham slabs. The doorsteps were worn into curves, and the ancient tiles which lined the porch were marked with the rebus of a cheese and a man, after the original builder. Within, the ceilings were corrugated with heavy oaken beams, and the uneven floors sagged into sharp curves. An odour of age and decay pervaded the whole crumbling building. There was one very large central room, into which

Ferguson led us. Here, in a huge old-fashioned fireplace with an iron screen behind it dated 1670, there blazed and spluttered a splendid log fire.

The room, as I gazed round, was a most singular mixture of dates and of places. The half-panelled walls may well have belonged to the original yeoman farmer of the seventeenth century. They were ornamented, however, on the lower part by a line of well-chosen modern water-colours; while above, where yellow plaster took the place of oak, there was hung a fine collection of South American utensils and weapons, which had been brought, no doubt, by the Peruvian lady upstairs. Holmes rose, with that quick curiosity which sprang from his eager mind, and examined them with some care. He returned with his eyes full of thought.

'Hullo!' he cried. 'Hullo!'

A spaniel had lain in a basket in the corner. It came slowly forward towards its master, walking with difficulty. Its hind-legs moved irregularly and its tail was on the ground. It licked Ferguson's hand.

'What is it, Mr. Holmes?'

'The dog. What's the matter with it?'

'That's what puzzled the vet. A sort of paralysis. Spinal meningitis, he thought. But it is passing. He'll be all right soon – won't you, Carlo?'

A shiver of assent passed through the drooping tail. The dog's mournful eyes passed from one of us to the other. He knew that we were discussing his case.

'Did it come on suddenly?'

'In a single night.'

'How long ago?'

'It may have been four months ago.'

'Very remarkable. Very suggestive.'

'What do you see in it, Mr. Holmes?'

'A confirmation of what I had already thought.'

'For God's sake, what *do* you think, Mr. Holmes? It may be a mere intellectual puzzle to you, but it is life and death to me! My wife a would-be murderer – my child in constant danger! Don't play with me, Mr. Holmes. It is too terribly serious.'

The big Rugby three-quarter was trembling all over. Holmes put his hand soothingly upon his arm.

'I fear that there is pain for you, Mr. Ferguson, whatever the solution may be,' said he. 'I would spare you all I can. I cannot say more for the instant, but before I leave this house I hope I may have something definite.'

'Please God you may! If you will excuse me, gentlemen, I will go up to my wife's room and see if there has been any change.'

He was away some minutes, during which Holmes resumed his examination of the curiosities upon the wall. When our host returned it was clear from his downcast face that he had made no progress. He brought with him a tall, slim, brown-faced girl.

'The tea is ready, Dolores,' said Ferguson. 'See that your mistress has everything she can wish.'

'She verra ill,' cried the girl, looking with indignant eyes at her master. 'She no ask for food. She verra ill. She need doctor. I frightened stay alone with her without doctor.'

Ferguson looked at me with a question in his eyes.

'I should be so glad if I could be of use.'

'Would your mistress see Dr. Watson?'

'I take him. I no ask leave. She needs doctor.'

'Then I'll come with you at once.'

I followed the girl, who was quivering with strong emotion, up the staircase and down an ancient corridor. At the end was an iron-clamped and massive door. It struck me as I looked at it that if Ferguson tried to force his way to his wife he would find it no easy matter. The girl drew a key from her pocket, and the heavy oaken planks creaked upon their old hinges. I passed in and she swiftly followed, fastening the door behind her.

On the bed a woman was lying who was clearly in a high fever. She was only half conscious, but as I entered she raised a pair of frightened but beautiful eyes and glared at me in apprehension. Seeing a stranger, she appeared to be relieved, and sank back with a sigh upon the pillow. I stepped up to her with a few reassuring words, and she lay still while I took her pulse and temperature. Both were high, and yet my impression was that the condition was rather that of mental and nervous excitement than of any actual seizure.

'She lie like that one day, two day. I 'fraid she die,' said the girl.

The woman turned her flushed and handsome face towards me.

'Where is my husband?'

'He is below, and would wish to see you.'

'I will not see him. I will not see him.' Then she seemed to wander off into delirium. 'A fiend! A fiend! Oh, what shall I do with this devil?'

'Can I help you in any way?'

'No. No one can help. It is finished. All is destroyed. Do what I will, all is destroyed.'

The woman must have some strange delusion. I could not see honest Bob Ferguson in the character of fiend or devil.

'Madame,' I said, 'your husband loves you dearly. He is deeply grieved at this happening.'

Again she turned on me those glorious eyes.

'He loves me. Yes. But do I not love him? Do I not love him even to sacrifice myself rather than break his dear heart. That is how I love him. And yet he could think of me – he could speak of me so.'

'He is full of grief, but he cannot understand.'

'No, he cannot understand. But he should trust.'

'Will you not see him?' I suggested.

'No, no; I cannot forget those terrible words nor the look upon his face. I will not see him. Go now. You can do nothing for me. Tell him only one thing. I want my child. I have a right to my child. That is the only message I can send him.' She turned her face to the wall and would say no more.

I returned to the room downstairs, where Ferguson and Holmes still sat by the fire. Ferguson listened moodily to my account of the interview.

'How can I send her the child?' he said. 'How do I know what strange impulse might come upon her? How can I ever forget how she rose from beside it with its blood upon her lips?' He shuddered at the recollection. 'The child is safe with Mrs. Mason, and there he must remain.'

A smart maid, the only modern thing which we had seen in the house, had brought in some tea. As she was serving it the door opened and a youth entered the room. He was a remarkable lad, pale-faced and fair-haired, with excitable light blue eyes which blazed into a sudden flame of emotion and joy as they rested upon his father. He rushed forward and threw his arms round his neck with the abandon of a loving girl.

'Oh, daddy,' he cried, 'I did not know that you were due yet. I should have been here to meet you. Oh, I am so glad to see you!'

Ferguson gently disengaged himself from the embrace with some little show of embarrassment.

'Dear old chap,' said he, patting the flaxen head with a very tender hand. 'I came early because my friends, Mr. Holmes and Dr. Watson, have been persuaded to come down and spend an evening with us.'

'Is that Mr. Holmes, the detective?'

'Yes.'

The youth looked at us with a very penetrating and, as it seemed to me, unfriendly gaze.

'What about your other child, Mr. Ferguson?' asked Holmes. 'Might we make the acquaintance of the baby?'

'Ask Mrs. Mason to bring baby down,' said Ferguson. The boy went off with a curious, shambling gait which told my surgical eyes that he was suffering from a weak spine. Presently he returned, and behind him came a tall, gaunt woman bearing in her arms a very beautiful child, dark-eyed, golden-haired, a wonderful mixture of the Saxon and the Latin. Ferguson was evidently devoted to it, for he took it into his arms and fondled it most tenderly.

'Fancy anyone having the heart to hurt him,' he muttered, as he glanced down at the small, angry red pucker upon the cherub throat.

It was at this moment that I chanced to glance at Holmes, and saw a most singular intentness in his expression. His face was as set as if it had been carved out of old ivory, and his eyes, which had glanced for a moment at father and child, were now fixed with eager curiosity upon something at the other side of the room. Following his gaze I could only guess that he was looking out through the window at the melancholy, dripping garden. It is true that a shutter had half closed outside and obstructed the view, but none the less it was certainly at the window that Holmes was fixing his concentrated attention. Then he smiled, and his eyes came back to the baby. On its chubby neck there was this small puckered mark. Without speaking, Holmes examined it with care.

Finally he shook one of the dimpled fists which waved in front of him.

'Good-bye, little man. You have made a strange start in life. Nurse, I should wish to have a word with you in private.'

He took her aside and spoke earnestly for a few minutes. I only heard the last words, which were: 'Your anxiety will soon, I hope, be set at rest.' The woman, who seemed to be a sour, silent kind of creature, withdrew with the child.

'What is Mrs. Mason like?' asked Holmes.

'Not very prepossessing externally, as you can see, but a heart of gold, and devoted to the child.'

'Do you like her, Jack?' Holmes turned suddenly upon the boy. His expressive mobile face shadowed over, and he shook his head.

'Jacky has very strong likes and dislikes,' said Ferguson, putting his arm round the boy. 'Luckily I am one of his likes.'

The boy cooed and nestled his head upon his father's breast. Ferguson gently disengaged him.

'Run away, little Jacky,' said he, and he watched his son with loving eyes until he disappeared. 'Now, Mr. Holmes,' he continued, when the boy was gone, 'I really feel that I have brought you on a fool's errand, for what can you possibly do, save give me your sympathy? It must be an exceedingly delicate and complex affair from your point of view.'

'It is certainly delicate,' said my friend, with an amused smile, 'but I have not been struck up to now with its complexity. It has been a case for intellectual deduction, but when this original intellectual deduction is confirmed point by point by quite a number of independent incidents, then the subjective becomes objective and we can say confidently that we have reached our goal. I had, in fact, reached it before we left Baker Street, and the rest has merely been observation and confirmation.'

Ferguson put his big hand to his furrowed forehead.

'For Heaven's sake, Holmes,' he said hoarsely, 'if you can see the truth in this matter, do not keep me in suspense. How do I stand? What shall I do? I care nothing as to how you have found your facts so long as you have really got them.'

'Certainly I owe you an explanation, and you shall have it. But you will permit me to handle the matter in my own way? Is the lady capable of seeing us, Watson?'

'She is ill, but she is quite rational.'

'Very good. It is only in her presence that we can clear the matter up. Let us go up to her.'

'She will not see me,' cried Ferguson.

'Oh, yes, she will,' said Holmes. He scribbled a few lines upon a sheet of paper. 'You at least have the *entrée*, Watson. Will you have the goodness to give the lady this note?'

I ascended again and handed the note to Dolores, who cautiously opened the door. A minute later I heard a cry from within, a cry in which joy and surprise seemed to be blended. Dolores looked out.

'She will see them. She will leesten,' said she.

At my summons Ferguson and Holmes came up. As we entered the room Ferguson took a step or two towards his wife, who had raised herself in the bed, but she held out her hand to repulse him. He sank into an arm-chair, while Holmes seated himself beside him, after bowing to the lady, who looked at him with wide-eyed amazement.

'I think we can dispense with Dolores,' said Holmes. 'Oh, very well, madame, if you would rather she stayed. I can see no objection. Now, Mr. Ferguson, I am a busy man with many calls, and my methods have to be short and direct. The swiftest surgery is the least painful. Let me first say what will ease your mind. Your wife is a very good, a very loving, and a very ill-used woman.' Ferguson sat up with a cry of joy.

'Prove that, Mr. Holmes, and I am your debtor for ever.'

'I will do so, but in doing so I must wound you deeply in another direction.'

'I care nothing so long as you clear my wife. Everything on earth is insignificant compared to that.'

'Let me tell you, then, the train of reasoning which passed through my mind in Baker Street. The idea of a vampire was to me absurd. Such things do not happen in criminal practice in England. And yet your observation was precise. You had seen the lady rise from beside the child's cot with the blood upon her lips.'

'I did.'

'Did it not occur to you that a bleeding wound may be sucked for some other purpose than to draw the blood from it? Was there not a Queen in English history who sucked such a wound to draw poison from it?'

'Poison!'

'A South American household. My instinct felt the presence of those weapons upon the wall before my eyes ever saw them. It might have been other poison, but that was what occurred to me. When I saw that little empty quiver beside the small bird-bow, it was just what I expected to see. If the child were pricked with one of those arrows dipped in curare or some other devilish drug, it would mean death if the venom were not sucked out.

'And the dog! If one were to use such a poison, would one not try it first in order to see that it had not lost its power? I did not foresee the dog, but at least I understood him and he fitted into my reconstruction.

'Now do you understand? Your wife feared such an attack. She saw it made and saved the child's life, and yet she shrank from telling you all the truth, for she knew how you loved the boy and feared lest it break your heart.'

'Jacky!'

'I watched him as you fondled the child just now. His face was clearly reflected in the glass of the window where the shutter formed a background. I saw such jealousy, such cruel hatred, as I have seldom seen in a human face.'

'My Jacky!'

'You have to face it, Mr. Ferguson. It is the more painful because it is a distorted love, a maniacal exaggerated love for you, and possibly for his dead mother, which has prompted his action. His very soul is consumed with hatred for this splendid child, whose health and beauty are a contrast to his own weakness.'

'Good God! It is incredible!'

'Have I spoken the truth, madame?'

The lady was sobbing, with her face buried in the pillows. Now she turned to her husband.

'How could I tell you, Bob? I felt the blow it would be to you. It was better that I should wait and that it should come from some other lips than mine. When this gentleman, who seems to have powers of magic, wrote that he knew all, I was glad.'

'I think a year at sea would be my prescription for Master Jacky,' said Holmes, rising from his chair.

'Only one thing is still clouded, madame. We can quite understand your attacks upon Master Jacky. There is a limit to a mother's patience. But how did you dare to leave the child these last two days?'

'I had told Mrs. Mason. She knew.'

'Exactly. So I imagined.'

Ferguson was standing by the bed, choking, his hands outstretched and quivering.

'This, I fancy, is the time for our exit, Watson,' said Holmes in a whisper. 'If you will take one elbow of the too faithful Dolores, I will take the other. There, now,' he added, as he closed the door behind him.

'I think we may leave them to settle the rest among themselves.'

I have only one further note of this case. It is the letter which Holmes wrote in final answer to that with which the narrative begins. It ran thus:

BAKER STREET,
Nov. 21*st.*

Re Vampires.

SIR,—

Referring to your letter of the 19th, I beg to state that I have looked into the inquiry of your client, Mr. Robert Ferguson, of Ferguson & Muirhead, tea brokers, of Mincing Lane, and that the matter has been brought to a satisfactory conclusion. With thanks for your recommendation,

I am, Sir,
Faithfully yours,
SHERLOCK HOLMES.

*   *   *

ARTHUR CONAN DOYLE was a Scottish doctor who filled in his spare time writing stories of crime and the supernatural until his creation of Sherlock Holmes in *A Study in Scarlet* first published in *Beeton's Christmas Annual* for 1887, set him on the way to becoming world famous. Ever since then, readers of all ages have enjoyed Holmes' exciting cases, with the novel, *The Hound of the Baskervilles* (1902) and 'The Sussex Vampire' (1924) the best of these with creepy, supernatural themes. Both have been filmed and adapted for television many times in the intervening years. The popularity of Conan Doyle's four novels and five collections of short stories about the super-sleuth has completely overshadowed his other fiction, in particular his tales of historical romance which he believed to be his best work. However, he became increasingly fascinated with ghosts and the supernatural during the later years of his life and spent a great deal of time and money investigating reports of hauntings and cases of the occult. He wrote about some of the spooky things that happened to him in a book called *The Edge of the Unknown* that was published in 1930 just before his death.

CLOUD COVER

Robert Swindells

Although it is only two weeks to Christmas, Laura is not looking forward to the festive season. She is very worried about her mother who used to be such a bundle of energy. Mum was always out doing things and the only time Laura ever saw her sit still was when she painted. But now she's been struck down with a virus which none of the doctors or specialists whom she's seen can even put a name to. When Laura notices a picture of a cloud-packed sky with the sun just about to burst through, hanging in a gallery window, she decides to buy it for her mum for Christmas, hoping it will cheer her up. But how on earth is she going to afford the price? Despite her misgivings, Laura is drawn to the gallery day after day and becomes aware of something scary happening. The scene is changing before her very eyes . . .

* * *

Laura dawdled along the High Street looking at the festive displays in shop windows. It was two weeks before Christmas. Last year at this time she'd already begun to feel that special excitement the approach of Christmas brings, but not this year. The street was festooned with coloured lights again, and the shops sparkled at least as cheerfully as they ever had, but Laura's spirits felt no lift.

It was Mum, of course. Last year at this time Mum had still been her old self, endlessly rushing around, always in a hurry. Meetings, painting classes, coffee mornings and dinner parties. Constantly on the phone. Never a dull moment and not enough hours in the day. Up until three months ago, it seemed the only time Mum sat down for longer than five minutes was when she was working at one of her delicate water-colours.

Then early in September the illness struck. It was quite sudden. One day she was hurtling about as usual, and the next her strength had deserted her so that it was as much as she could manage to walk slowly from her bedroom to the bathroom and back. A virus, the doctor had said. Two weeks, three at the most and she'd be fine, but she wasn't. Not in September, nor October, nor November. In November Dad had taken Mum to see a specialist. At the hospital they'd done tests. All sorts of tests. They could find nothing wrong, but something *was* wrong. Something without a name.

Now Mum hardly ever came downstairs, and she never, ever went out. She spent a lot of the time sleeping, and when she was awake she'd sit propped on pillows with her eyes closed, listening to the radio. Now and then she'd try to read but reading made her nauseous, and of course she couldn't paint at all. She'd become a different person, and Laura found this both frightening and unutterably sad. It was why she was dawdling on her way from school where once she might have flown, and why the approach of Christmas had lost its power to thrill her.

The last shop on the row was The Gallery, where framed prints of famous pictures shared the window with original works by local painters. Laura always stopped to look in this window. She paused now, gazing through the dusty pane at the dozen or so prints and paintings on display. No tinsel glittered in this window. There was no plastic holly, no artificial snow. The window looked much as it did all the year round, and in fact Laura had seen all of the pictures before, except one.

The new painting was a water-colour. As Laura's eyes came to rest on it she gasped. An ache started in her chest and spread into her throat and for a moment she felt she might cry.

It was sky mostly, but such a sky! Wide, wild and wind-wracked it was, cloud-clogged and bruised-looking. As she gazed, Laura could *feel* the wind which drove those clouds, shredding them, spreading them in rags across the bare, blasted moorland hinted at in the bottom third of the picture. She shivered, imagining herself for a moment standing alone in the midst of that howling moor, and she knew that if her mother saw this picture she would long to possess it.

For an instant, Laura's heart soared. She would buy the painting, carry it home wrapped in brown paper, hide it till Christmas morning and then . . . She saw Mum's face, heard her gasp as she herself had gasped. She'd be happy, wouldn't she? For a while anyway. They'd *both* be happy.

Then she saw the price tag and moaned softly to herself. Ninety pounds. Tears of disappointment pricked her eyes. She didn't have ninety pounds. Even Dad didn't have ninety pounds – not to spend on pictures, anyway. The painting was an original of course, hence the price, but still . . .

Oh, what's the use? It was as much as Laura could do to tear her eyes away but she turned and walked on. It's not fair, she thought. Mum's so ill, and that picture would've given her a bit of happiness on Christmas Day. Is that so much to ask? Is it?

There was a coffee shop on the corner of the next block. Laura had never been inside but now, on impulse, she pushed open the glass door. She knew why she was doing it and the knowledge made her feel guilty. The fact was, she didn't want to go home to a house tainted with her father's pessimism, the faint smell of sickness, the shadow of defeat. She bought a cup of coffee and carried it to a corner table. Except for herself and the girl behind the counter, the place was empty. Laura sat with her hands wrapped round the cup, thinking about the painting and about her mother. So distracted was she that she didn't realise she was crying, or that another person had entered the shop, till a shadow fell across her and a soft arm descended on her thin shoulders.

'Now, now, dear, whatever's the matter?'

'Huh?' Laura looked up, groping in her pocket for a tissue. Her comforter was a smartish woman of middle age with short, iron-grey hair. 'Oh – I'm sorry. I didn't know I was – I'm all right now.'

'Are you sure?' The woman sat down. 'Perhaps you'd like more coffee?'

'Oh, no. Honestly, I'm fine. Feeling a bit sorry for myself, that's all.'

The woman gazed at her. 'Sometimes it helps to talk, you know – even to a stranger. Why don't you tell me all about it, dear?'

She didn't want to. She didn't see how talking could help at all, but the woman had a soothing voice and sympathetic eyes and in five minutes Laura had told her everything. When she'd finished, her listener looked into her eyes and asked, 'And how do you feel now?'

Laura smiled briefly. 'A bit better.' To her surprise, this was true.

The woman nodded. 'There you are, you see? No trouble's so big it won't shrink with sharing.' She smiled. 'Your mother *will* be well again, Laura.'

Laura gazed at her. 'How can you be so sure?'

'Trust me.' She signalled to the waitress and ordered coffee for two. She didn't speak again till it was on the table, then she said, 'I know it seems impossible at the moment, Laura, but the clouds will blow away. They always do. All we have to do is keep going till the sun shines again.' She smiled. 'Drink your coffee, dear.'

Laura nodded and lifted her cup. How clever, she

thought, to talk in terms of clouds and sunshine when she knows my mind is full of that fantastic picture!

It seemed neither of them had anything further to say, because they sipped in silence. When the woman excused herself a few minutes later and rose to leave, Laura said, 'Thanks for listening. I really do feel better. I mean it.'

The woman nodded, smiling. 'I know you do. Goodbye, Laura, and remember – look for the sun.'

'Where have you been?' Laura's father demanded as she walked into the house. 'It's twenty past five.' He was frying something, filling the kitchen with a pungent blue haze which made her feel sick.

'Nowhere. I was looking at the shops.'

'Well, I wish you'd come straight home, Laura. There's plenty to do around here with me working all hours and your mother . . . the way she is.'

'I know, Dad. I *do* come straight home, usually. It was just this once – the Christmas lights and all that. How *is* Mum?'

Her father sighed. 'The same. Go and sit with her, there's a love. I'll call you when dinner's ready.'

Laura pulled a face. 'I'm not hungry, Dad, thanks. I had something earlier.'

Her father shrugged, busy with a fish-slice. 'Suit yourself. They say eleven's a funny age. I expect you imagine you're getting fat or something.'

Laura went upstairs. Her mother, propped on pillows, was finishing her meal. She smiled. 'Hello, Laura. Good day at school?'

Laura smiled wryly. 'Did *you* ever have a good day at school, Mum?'

Her mother chuckled. 'I suppose not, dear – not at the time. It's when you look back it all seems to have been such fun.'

'Well,' said Laura, 'all I can say, is, I'll be glad when *I'm* looking back at my schooldays.'

Her mother smiled gently. 'Then I hope you won't find yourself looking back from where I'm sitting, darling.'

'Oh, Mum! I didn't mean . . .'

'No, I know you didn't, sweetheart. What I mean is, don't be wishing your time away. Enjoy what you have *now*, because we never know what the future has in store for us.'

That night, curled in her bed, Laura thought about her mother's words. Enjoy what you have now. But that's just it, Mum – I can't, because all the time at the back of my mind is *you*! Your illness, your rotten fate – and it spoils everything. Oh, I know it's happening to you not me, and I know it's selfish, but sometimes I can't help seeing it as *my* bad luck because it's messing up my life too!

Laura rolled over and cried quietly into her pillow. Just before she slept she saw the wild ragged sky in the picture and a voice in her head murmured, 'Look for the sun.'

Next day Laura felt tired at school. They were preparing for the festive celebrations, learning a new carol and rehearsing their play, but try as she might she couldn't enter into the spirit of things. She kept thinking about the picture, and the woman's words. 'I *am* looking,' she caught herself whispering more than once. 'I'm looking for the sun.' She didn't usually talk to herself. It occurred to her that she might be going mad, and at breaktime when Sandra Robinson asked her how her mother was, she burst into tears.

The afternoon dragged, but at last it was three-thirty and Laura set off home, taking a circuitous route to avoid Sandra Robinson. She was headed for The Gallery and she wanted to be alone when she got there. Why this was important – why she had to go there at all – Laura didn't know. All she knew was, she'd been thinking about the picture all day and praying it would still be in the window.

It was. There were shoppers all around but Laura didn't see them. She stood at the window, making a visor of her cupped hands to cut reflection, and there it was – the sky which had got into her head somehow and a wind you could *see*, raging over the moor. She felt again that ache, that lift towards tears. 'Oh, Mum!' she murmured. 'How I wish . . .' She broke off, staring more intently at the picture. She could have sworn she'd taken it all in yesterday, every detail, yet now she noticed something she hadn't seen then. There was a place in the cloudscape where light seemed to penetrate as a faint, suffused glow, as if somewhere beyond those dark accumulations of vapour the sun might be shining. It was beautifully done – she remembered having seen skies just like

that – and of course it must have been there yesterday, only she hadn't noticed. Oh, but how could I *not*
have noticed? she wondered. It's the centre, surely –
the whole *point* of the picture! How could I possibly
have missed it?

She stood gazing, her breath making a fogged disc
on the glass till the cold in her feet broke the spell.
She looked at her watch and groaned. Twenty past
four. More hassle from Dad if he's home. She moved
quickly, threading her way through the tea-time
crowd. Passing the coffee shop she glanced through
its brightly lit window but the woman wasn't there
and Laura felt vaguely disappointed.

When she got home, her father wasn't in yet. She
went upstairs briefly to her mother, then hurried
downstairs to cook. At least today there'd be no
bluish haze. To her own surprise she caught herself
smiling at this thought, and she hummed as she
dumped pasta in boiling water and chopped a winter
salad. Dad came in while she was doing this and
smiled at her, which was something. Maybe, she
mused, mixing oil and vinegar in a teacup, maybe
I'm beginning to feel Christmassy after all. It's a little
late this year but they do say better late than never.

Laura slept a little better that night, though her
dreams were once more filled with stormy skies and a
voice which spoke of the sun.

Mornings fell into a pattern. Seven o'clock: up, wash,
dress. Look in on Mum, act cheerful. Down to the
kitchen where Dad's had breakfast and is about to
leave for work.

'Morning, Dad.'

'Morning love. Don't forget Mum's breakfast, will you?'

'No, Dad.'

'And do try to wash the dishes before you leave the house – the place was a pigsty when I got in yesterday.'

'Yes, Dad.'

'Oh – and remember to call at Tesco's on your way home, love. We're nearly out of bread.'

'Okay, Dad.'

'You'd better write it down now so you don't forget.'

'Yes, Dad.'

'And Laura?'

'What is it, Dad?'

'Give us a smile of a morning, eh? It's depressing enough around here without *you* standing there with a face as long as a fiddle.'

'Sorry, Dad.'

'Yes, well – you'd better get on or you'll be making yourself late for school again.'

'Yes, Dad.'

''Bye then – see you tonight.'

''Bye!'

Eight-thirty. 'I'm off now, Mum.'

'Righto, darling. Got a tissue?'

'Yes, Mum.'

'Lunch money?'

'Yes, Mum.'

'Money for Tesco?'

'Yes, Mum.'

'Left the place tidy for Dad, have you? You know how he fusses.'

'Yes, Mum.'

'Check everything's switched off before you go, won't you? And don't forget the bread.'

'Okay, Mum.'

'Have a nice day, dear.'

'Sure, Mum – you too.'

At twenty to four that afternoon Tesco seethed with glassy-eyed shoppers anaesthetised with piped carols and force-fed on Christmas, trundling laden trolleys between inflatable reindeer and chocolate Santas with a bare minimum of goodwill to all men. Laura grabbed bread, added a bunch of yellow chrysanths for her mother, and checked out.

Outside, she hurried along the darkening street. The plastic carrier kept banging against her leg and she hoped she wasn't wrecking the flowers. She reached The Gallery, dropped the bag between her feet and peered through the window.

There. It *is* there, the light. Definitely. I didn't just imagine it. In fact . . . She shielded her eyes as before and peered more closely. It's stronger, surely? I mean, if it was *this* noticeable I wouldn't have missed it the first time, would I? It's stronger *and* more extensive. That whole passage left of centre is positively luminous, as though the sun might break through at any second. It was nothing like that before. It was dark. Those clouds were scowling at you as if to say, there'll be no sun today or any other day – the sun's dead. So how –?

Laura swallowed hard and shook her head. Water-colours don't change, yet this one has. Twice. Maybe it's changing all the time, slowly, like an hour-hand moving round. I'd like to stay here and watch but I can't, can I? I can't. She glanced at her watch. Five past four. All I can do is come again tomorrow.

There was something cooking but no car on the drive when she got home. Funny, thought Laura – Dad must've been home and gone out again. She opened the oven door. It was some sort of casserole and it smelled good. Bit ambitious for Dad. She unpacked her shopping, stuck the chrysanths in a vase, ran water into it and carried it upstairs. Her mother turned her head on the pillow and smiled as she entered the room. 'Hello, darling!'

'Hi, Mum. I brought you these. Where's Dad?'

'They're gorgeous, darling. Thank you. Put them over here where I can see them. Your father's not back from work yet.'

'But the oven's on, Mum. Something's cooking. Who –?'

Her mother laughed. 'Me, Laura. I put it on. It's a chicken casserole.'

'*You*, Mum?'

'Yes, me. I felt amazingly well for a time this afternoon – felt this sudden burst of energy – so I got up and cooked. Aren't you pleased?'

'Pleased?' Laura bent and hugged her mother. 'I'm not just pleased, Mum – I'm megachuffed! I'd begun to think we'd never see you out of bed again.' She straightened. 'How d'you feel now?'

Her mother shrugged. 'A little tired, dear – but also chuffed.' She chuckled. 'Not megachuffed, mind you – that'll be tomorrow – but there's definitely an element of chuff about me, and I'm cultivating it.'

That evening was easily the best since September. Her brief spell in the kitchen had boosted Mum enormously, and when Dad learned of it he perked up too. For the first time in months, Laura went to bed happy.

As she settled down she remembered the words of the woman in the coffee shop and smiled. All we have to do is keep going till the sun shines again. Well, she'd been right, whoever she was. Laura had kept going – just – and this evening the sun had definitely shone. Trouble was, thinking about the woman led on to thinking about the picture, and once she started thinking about that she couldn't get it out of her head.

They don't change. It's impossible. When I'm there – right there at that window – it's *obvious* the thing's different from last time, but thinking about it afterwards I know I must be mistaken. I know the woman talked about clouds and sunshine, but that had to be because I'd just described the picture to her. I don't remember describing it – I thought I told her about it without giving any details – but I must have. The only possible explanation otherwise is that she's psychic, and I don't believe in that stuff, and I don't believe in magic pictures either, so there has to be a rational explanation. But what?

Laura wrestled with the question till her eyes burned with tiredness and her sheets grew damp and wrinkled. It must have been midnight when it hit her. Of course! She sat up and gulped water from the glass on her bedside unit. Monet. Claude Monet. The haystacks. Now, why didn't I think of that before? Monet saw two haystacks in a field and he decided to make a painting of them, only he didn't do just *one* painting – he did four. Or was it five? Anyway, what he did was, he painted the haystacks the way they looked in the early morning, then did them again later when the light had changed and the shadows fell differently, and so on. The last painting showed the two haystacks at sunset. All of the paintings showed the same haystacks, but each painting was different in all sorts of ways because of the light. And that's what somebody's done with my cloudscape! They've made a series of paintings, showing what happens when a cloudy day turns into a sunny one. It's the artist's equivalent of the slow-motion sequence you get on the telly.

Yes, that's it! I haven't been seeing things and I'm not going barmy. Whoever owns The Gallery has this cloud-scape series, and they're displaying them one by one. Tomorrow, just to make sure, I'm going to pop in and ask, but I know I'm right.

Laura lay down, smiled and fell asleep. Rational explanations are always comforting, even if they're not always correct.

The next day was a good one for Laura. She'd slept well, Mum had seemed quite chirpy over her breakfast tray and there was no more mystery attached to the picture. Sandra Robinson didn't ask how Mum was but Laura told her anyway. Better, thanks. Much, much better. Just to say the words made her feel good. The school looked pretty in tinsel, the carol was coming along fine and the hours flew. And when three-thirty rolled around it was great to set off home and not wish you were going somewhere else instead. She even felt like going *straight* home. After all, she didn't *have* to stop at The Gallery. It wasn't as though she was going to buy the flipping picture, was it? Fat chance. But on the other hand, hadn't she stayed awake half the night wrestling with the mystery? Hadn't she cracked it? Well, then – she was entitled to the satisfaction of having the correctness of her solution confirmed, and it'd only take a few minutes, right? Right.

She arrived at twenty to four. There were plenty of shoppers about. Laura hoped none of them would come in The Gallery while she was inside. It was going to be hard enough without someone barging in halfway through. She'd looked in the window hundreds of times but had never been in. There was a glass panel in the door, but a casual glance wouldn't show you much. The interior always seemed dark, and you wondered how customers could possibly examine the pictures they meant to buy. The window was attractive enough if you liked to look at paintings, but there was nothing inviting about the shop itself.

Laura looked in the window and saw that yesterday's cloudscape had been replaced by the next in the series. Yesterday there'd been a bright, almost pulsating glow in the vapour left of centre. It was so beautifully painted you *knew* the sun was about to break through – you could feel it out here on the December street – but it hadn't happened yet.

In today's picture, it had. The glow was still there, burning out of the haze, but now a single pale shaft of sunlight fell vertically from the cloud's dark belly on to a distant hillside. Laura saw how with one deft brushstroke the artist had bestowed luminosity on that hillside. It was a green-gold smear a centimetre long, yet it drew both the eye and the memory. You'd seen hillsides with the sun on them and they looked so *exactly* like that it made you want to weep.

No. Laura tore her moist eyes away. No blubbing. You don't have ninety pounds and that's that. It's time. Up the step, through the door, ask your question, home to Mum. Easy.

It wasn't easy, though. She hesitated on the step, trying to see through the dark panel, half hoping a customer would show up and give her an excuse to abandon her plan. From out here it looked like the sort of shop you sometimes see in horror movies – the sort where when you go in, a rusty bell pings and an ugly old guy comes shuffling through a dusty curtain and you just *know* he's going to turn out to be a zombie or a vampire or an alien or something, and when you try to leave the shop the door's locked and he's coming towards you, grinning a snaggle-tooth grin.

Don't be so stupid! It's a perfectly ordinary little shop on a busy street in a boring English town where nothing ever happens. It's probably run by a money-grubbing little wally with two chins and a ginger moustache who drives a Volvo and collects concrete gnomes.

So how come I've *never* seen anyone go inside?

Laura dismissed the question, took a deep breath, grabbed the door handle and pushed. There was no bell, rusty or otherwise, and nobody came through the curtain. The proprietor was already behind the counter, beaming. It was the woman who'd bought her coffee.

'Oh – hello – I –'

'Laura.' The woman smiled. 'You've come for your picture at last.'

'No – no.' Laura shook her head. 'I told you. I don't have ninety pounds. I came in to ask something, only I didn't know this was your shop.'

The woman arched her brows. 'Does it make a difference?'

'I – guess not.'

'Then ask.'

'Well, it's just – there's more than one picture, isn't there? I mean, there *has* to be because water-colours don't change, only I thought – for a day or two

I thought it *was* changing. Either that or I was going mad.'

The woman looked at her. 'I'm sorry, Laura – I'm afraid I haven't the faintest idea what you're talking about. I have hundreds of pictures here but there's only the one cloud-scape.'

'Are – are you sure?'

'Am I sure?' The woman chuckled. 'I ought to be, dear – I painted it.'

'You?' gasped Laura.

'Why not me?' The woman seemed amused. 'Don't I look like a painter?'

'Oh, no. I mean, yes. It's not that. I mean – look, I was so sure I'd cracked the mystery, and now –'

'Mystery?' The woman shook her head. 'There's no mystery, Laura. I painted a cloudscape. A *single* cloudscape. It's been in my window all week. If you've seen changes, it's the way you've looked at the picture that's changed.' She smiled. 'Shall I wrap it for you? How *is* your mother, by the way?'

Laura shook her head. 'No. I haven't got the money, you see. Mum's better, thanks. Much better.'

'Good. I'm glad. And since it's my painting – my own work, I mean – the money doesn't matter, does it?' She began pulling brown paper from a roll bolted to the counter.

'Oh, please!' protested Laura. 'I can't do that. I can't take your picture and not pay. It wouldn't be right.'

The woman shook her head. 'Then don't take it, dear – let me give it to you.' She fetched the painting, placed it on the paper and began wrapping it. 'I don't have giftwrap, I'm afraid.'

'It doesn't – I still don't feel right about this.'

'Don't let it worry you, Laura. It's my pleasure, believe me. Here.' She held out the neat rectangular package. Laura took it.

'Thank you. I – I'll never forget this, honestly I won't. I don't even know your name.'

The woman shook her head. 'I know you don't and you're absolutely right – you'll never forget. Good-bye, Laura. Oh, and don't worry about your mother, dear – illness is a thing of the past for her now.'

Laura walked homeward in a warm haze of well-being. Not only could she *feel* Christmas – it seemed to her that she was included as never before at the very heart and meaning of the festival. She'd stopped believing in angels at around the same time as she'd realised there was no Santa Claus, but now her certainty regarding these matters faltered. It seemed to her she'd discovered one or the other, or maybe a combination of the two, running a poky little picture shop in the High Street. It wasn't till she turned the corner into her own road that she discovered how mistaken she was.

There were two fire engines, one ambulance, a haze of bluish smoke and a knot of people by the gate. Not our gate, said Laura's brain. Next door, surely? Nevertheless her pace quickened, and by the time her father intercepted her she knew and was running, half-blind with terror and with tears, towards her gutted home.

'Laura!' He circled her with his arms, forced her to halt, crushed her face against his shirt and tie. 'Wait, darling. You mustn't go near. There's nothing to be done.'

She cried out, writhing to break his hold. 'Mum? Is it Mum?'

She felt his affirmative nod. 'She was – she must have tried to cook, Laura,' he said. 'Collapsed in the kitchen. Mrs Atkinson saw smoke, but by then –'

'Is she –'

Again the affirmative nod.

'It's my fault, Dad. All my fault. If I'd come straight home instead of going to –' She broke off as the woman's last words came back to her. *Don't worry about your mother, dear – illness is a thing of the past for her now.*

'The picture – let me look at the picture!'

Her father struggled to restrain her but now she was wild. Desperate. When wriggling failed to free her she sank her teeth in his wrist, broke away and backed off, tearing at the wrapping. He made a grab for her but she sidestepped. The paper fell away to reveal what she'd known it concealed – a sombre, brooding cloudscape beyond which, somewhere, the sun lay dead.

She knew what she must do. She turned, clutching the picture, and began running back the way she'd come. She must find the woman – make her paint the sun! One stroke – one deft stroke was all it would take, then Mum would be all right again and Christmas could begin.

She couldn't know that already The Gallery stood empty, its window bare except for a square of card on which were scrawled the words FOR SALE.

*   *   *

ROBERT SWINDELLS has been called the master of spooky suspense and has won many awards for his scary novels including the Carnegie Medal for *Stone Cold* (1993) and an honour he shares only with Roald Dahl of twice winning the Children's Book Award with *Brother in the Land* (1984) and *Room 13* (1989). His stories deal with a variety of subjects, often with a mystical, unexplained theme, ranging from the weird floating monsters in a tank in *Hydra* (1991) to ghostly beings in an old railway tunnel in *The Thousand Eyes of Night* (1993). He also likes to base his stories on his own experiences, and his own favourite book, *Room 13*, was based on a school trip to Whitby in Yorkshire. 'One of the children told me I should write a story about the hotel where we were staying because one of the rooms was supposed to be haunted by Dracula!'

The author left school at fifteen and worked as a copyholder on a local paper before joining the RAF at seventeen for three years. He was then a clerk, an engineer and a printer before training and working as a teacher. What was to become his first published book began life as a thesis for his teacher training finals at Huddersfield Polytechnic. Robert Swindells' fascination with weird events plus his love for the classic horror stories which he had read as a child, all coupled to his ability to tell scary stories soon enabled him to become a full-time writer. But he has never lost his contact with youngsters. 'I keep up with their slang and what interests them,' he says. He also claims to have actually met a ghost: 'I had a favourite uncle who was a gunner on a Lancaster Bomber during the Second World War. One night when I was just falling asleep, the door to my bedroom slowly opened and there was Uncle Arthur with his thumbs up. I jumped out of bed and ran straight to my mother, shouting, "Where's Uncle Arthur?" She later told me his plane had been shot down from the sky and he'd died – *just three days before.*'

THE GHOST HORSE OF GENGHIS KHAN

Russell Hoban

John's father is also very sick. He's in hospital recovering from a heart attack. While he's away, John likes to spend time in his dad's study. It's full of books and videos that he uses for his writing. There are also shadowy places full of other exciting things including a human skeleton that makes eerie sounds when it is moved. But what fascinates John most of all is a pile of books all about the Mongol Empire and the most famous of all their warriors, Genghis Khan. His dad had obviously been using these because there is an unfinished story about the famous horseman still in his typewriter. But when John starts to dream about Genghis Khan and his dreams and reality get all mixed up, he's in for a very scary experience . . .

*   *   *

John was eight years old and he liked to be in his father's study. It was full of books and all kinds of things that his father needed for his writing. Sometimes after school John would lie on the oriental carpet and draw. Sometimes he would sit in the reading chair and read or look at videotapes that he listened to with headphones while his father worked.

There were shadowy places and lamplit places in the study. There were maps on the wall. There was a human skeleton that made gentle clacking sounds when you moved it. There were three pendulum clocks that struck the hours at different times when they were running. Now they were stopped at different times. There was a model of a Portuguese fishing boat, there was a stuffed barn owl. There were rocks and seashells from many places and a stone from a Crusader fort in Galilee with chisel marks on it. John ran his thumb over the chisel marks and thought of the hand that had held the chisel long ago. He held the left hand of the skeleton and moved its arm.

Among the clutter on the desk were some books with markers in them: *The Mongol Empire; The Mongols; The Devil's Horsemen; The Secret History of the Mongols.* John read bits here and there about Genghis Khan. He looked at drawings of thirteenth-century Mongol horsemen twisting in the saddle to shoot arrows. He read how Mongol children learned to ride before they could walk, how the warriors slept on horseback, how they drank the milk of their mares or opened a vein in a horse's leg to drink the blood.

'Genghis Khan,' he said aloud. He was alone in the lamplight and the shadows of the study. His father was in hospital, recovering from heart surgery. He slept wired to a cardiac monitor, his heartbeat regularly repeating its line of jagged peaks across the screen.

Genghis Khan, said John's mind. The mind was much older than the boy, it was as ancient as the stars, it remembered all sorts of things that John had never known. It was curious about everything and it was playful, it was obsessed with names and the sounds of words: Khwarizm; Khurasan; Karakorum; Genghis Khan. Genghis, Genghis, Genghis, it said, Genghis galloping, galloping. The thudding of unshod hooves is in the name; the bending of the bow is in the name, the bow of horn and sinew and lacquer. The rider twisting in the saddle draws the bowstring back and looses the arrow, the hiss of the hungry arrow cleaving time and darkness, cleaving forgetfulness so that the galloping of the ghost horse of Genghis Khan is fresh and strong in me.

The Mongols lived in tents, in yurts, thought John. My father and I have never slept in a tent. He sits at his desk writing except when he's napping or watching TV. He goes up and down the stairs slowly. I wonder what he was like when he was young. Did he ever gallop, did he ever have a bow and arrows?

In his father's typewriter was an unfinished page two. On the copyholder beside the typewriter was page one. It was headed: THE GHOST HORSE OF GENGHIS KHAN. John read:

Genghis Khan, the name lives its own life apart from the man who was whatever he was. Genghis, Genghis, Genghis Khan galloping, galloping in the long night. Hundreds of horses he must have ridden in his warrior lifetime and now he lies no one knows where and all the hundreds of horses have become one shape of galloping in the long night.

What colour is this galloping?

Red.

Is there a particular red horse?

There is now: a red roan with a white nose.

Is there a story about him?

Yes, I see it happening.

What do you see?

Here is Genghis Khan before he was Genghis Khan, when he was young, when he was called Temujin. Here he is, galloping for his life on the red roan. A close-coupled leggy horse, a clever-looking horse, a steadfast one, galloping, galloping. Behind him on the tawny steppe drifts the dust cloud of his going and through the dust gallop three riders hot on his track. Temujin has an arrow in his right shoulder, he cannot use his bow, nothing can save him but his horse. He leans low over its neck, he sees its eye roll back as the red roan listens for his voice.

'O thou of two worlds,' says Temujin. He doesn't know why he says this, he thinks of nothing, the words alone fill his mind, the surging gallop of the red roan is like a prayer wheel. On and on it gallops through the long afternoon, on and on until a long, long shudder . . .

There the unfinished page two ended. What do you think? said John's mind.

About what? said John.

About what's happening in the story, said his mind.

I'd rather not say, said John.

Three o'clock in the morning, said the three stopped clocks.

John looked at his watch. That isn't the time, he said. It's not even eight o'clock at night, it's not even my bedtime.

Not even your bedtime, said the clocks. Not all that much time though. For what? said John.

It isn't for us to say, said the clocks.

John pushed the typewriter carriage return and the unfinished page moved up two spaces. That's not the end of the story, said his mind.

Time to get ready for bed,' said his mother, and John went upstairs. His mother kissed him good night and he fell asleep and his mind began to speak to him again.

What is the shape of the galloping of the ghost horse of Genghis Khan? it said. Not of the eye, not to be seen, shadow of a memory, hoofbeats on the plains of here and gone. Here and gone, thought John in his sleep. Two places. Is there a drum, said his mind, is there a rattle, is there a bone whistle? How does one call up the ghost horse of Genghis Khan? Out of the herds of the dead, out of the shadows and the dust and the silence, out of the white pages of scholars and the smell of ink how does one call up that moving shadow on the screen of memory?

If you call me I will come, said the ghost horse.

Where are you? said John.

In your mind, said the ghost horse. In the shadows and the long night and the herds of the dead.

I don't know your name, said John. How can I call you if I don't know your name?

My name is not a name, said the ghost horse. Call me how you can. Call me and I will come.

What is it to be alive? said the sleeping John. What is it to be dead?

Ideas never die, said the ghost horse. I am an idea.

John woke up and went into his father's study. He turned on the lamps so that the places of lamplight and shadow appeared in their proper order. Three o'clock in the morning, said the three stopped clocks.

John looked at his watch. That's not the time, he said. It's only a little past two. Only a little past two, said the clocks. John looked at them very hard. They were telling the right time. He wound them and started them going. Then he sat down at the typewriter.

The unfinished page seemed to move in its blank whiteness, seemed to dance in its blankness before him. In that dancing was the red roan galloping, galloping until a long, long shudder broke its rhythm. In everything, said his mind, there is the animal of itself, the animal beyond the moment, beyond all moments. In the horse and in the man and in the boy, the animal of itself galloping, galloping.

John felt the dancing in the paper move towards him as he moved towards it. I'm not as good at stories as my father is, he said.

It isn't a question of being good at stories, said his mind. It's a question of how far you'll go.

At three o'clock in the morning in the hospital ward the pattern on the cardiac monitor lost its regularity and jumbled into random peaks and valleys. The staff nurse flung the pillows off John's father's bed and began to massage his chest while a student nurse gave him mouth-to-mouth respiration. The night sister dialled 222, said, 'Cardiac arrest!' and ran for the emergency trolley. 'Crash!' said the bleepers as the student started a bicarbonate drip while the staff nurse put an airway into John's father's throat and attached a re-breather bag. When the crash team arrived the anaesthetist inserted an endotracheal tube, put John's father on oxygen, and took over the re-breather. The doctor at the defibrillator applied the electrode jelly and said, 'Stand back.' He pressed the paddles against John's father's chest and delivered a 400-joule shock; John's father arched convulsively but the random peaks and valleys continued on the monitor screen. 'Stand back,' said the doctor, and did it again.

What did you say? said John to his mind.

I said it's a question of how far you'll go.

John wasn't aware of answering but he must have said something, thought something. There was a horrendous rushing, ripping, rending sound, a searing blast of pain as all before and after tore away from him and all the clocks struck three.

He whirled through blackness, wheeled high up into clear blue air and scanned the tawny steppe below him, saw the dry dust drifting, saw the horses and their riders strung out on the lion-coloured plain. Their shadows raced in silence over pebbles, blades of grass, old hoofprints. In the distance stood the wrinkled silent mountains, intolerably real.

Then the ground swooped close and blurred back under him in utter silence, he was in the galloping, in the animal of it. On and on he galloped; an immense fatigue dragged at him and there came a long, long shudder but the animal of him left all else behind, the animal of him became its motion, became the never-tiring motion of itself as sounds rushed in upon him, the incessant rhythmic thudding of his galloping hooves. He felt the weight of his rider, felt his own unending strength become a long, long rocking like the sea and far away.

In the hospital his father opened his eyes. 'O thou of two worlds,' he said.

'How are you feeling?' said the night sister.

'I almost didn't get here.'

'Tell me about it.'

'I felt my horse sink underneath me, then . . .'

'Then what?'

John's father laughed. 'It was a dream,' he said.

It was almost four o'clock in the morning when John's mother woke up and went into the study. She saw her son asleep at the desk with his head cradled on his arms. She read the page in the typewriter that had ended: '. . . on and on until a long, long shudder . . .' Now there was more. She read:

> . . . on and on until a long, long shudder passes through the horse but it doesn't stumble, it keeps

on galloping. The pursuers have no more arrows and they stop chasing Temujin.

It was getting dark when the red roan brought Temujin to his camp. His brother Khasar pulled out the arrow and bandaged the wound and got him a fresh horse. It was time to move camp, and they rode away. Temujin's wound hurt, he'd lost a lot of blood. He fell asleep in the saddle.

When he woke up the moon was shining and they were up in the hills. The horses were put out to graze and he went to look for the red roan but he couldn't find it.

'Where's the red roan?' he asked Khasar.

'How should I know?' said Khasar.

'But I rode into camp on it,' said Temujin.

'I found you lying on the ground at the edge of camp and there was no horse,' said Khasar.

'Were there any tracks?'

'No tracks.'

Then Temujin knew that the red roan had galloped beyond death to save him.

In two weeks John's father came home. He sat down at his desk and looked at the page in his typewriter. 'Someone's been typing on my page,' he said.

'It was me,' said John. 'I woke up in the middle of the night and came in here and I sort of had a dream at your desk.'

'Sleeptyping?' said his father.

'Something like that,' said John.

'It's not bad,' said his father. 'Not bad at all.'

*   *   *

RUSSELL HOBAN is an American author who has settled in England and was recently described as 'a children's writer for grown-ups'. He earned a world-wide audience of younger readers with his master-piece, *The Mouse and his Child* (1967), about two clockwork creatures who travel around endlessly try-ing to find a way that they no longer need to be wound-up to function. The success of the book led to an animated film in 1977. In the 1970s, Russell Hoban began writing novels for adults and his tale of *Riddley Walker* (1980) about a holocaust in southern England in the near future received the John W. Campbell Memorial Award.

The author started his working life in 1951 as an illustrator and moved on to become a copywriter in advertising and television. His first book, a work of non-fiction, *What Does It Do and How Does It Work?* (1959) combined his love of mechanical things with his skill as an artist. This was followed by the *Frances* series about a badger child, that was launched in 1960 with *Bedtime for Frances*. Among his later books, several have fantasy themes including the adult nov-els *Pilgermann* (1983) featuring an eleventh-century man who inhabits various eras in the form of ghosts, and *The Medusa Frequency* (1987) based on the myth of Orpheus and the Medusa; plus two of his stories for younger readers, *The Serpent Tower* (1983) and *Jim Hedgehog's Supernatural Christmas* (1992).

HOW 7 WENT MAD

Bram Stoker

Tineboy is the most unusual child in this book. He actually lives in a land of fantasy, 'Under The Sunset', with his pet raven, Mr Daw. It is a curious place full of dense forests, high mountains, castles and towns which the people can only leave in their dreams during the 'Rest Time'! Even the schools – like the one that Tineboy goes to – are very different from normal schools. At Tineboy's there is a teacher who loves to tell stories about the most extraordinary people – such as the Alphabet Doctor whose job is to look after the health of the letters of the alphabet! When the teacher tells this story to his class something really peculiar happens to the number 7 and Tineboy finds himself caught up in a series of events that just get more and more bizarre . . .

*   *   *

The Country Under The Sunset is a strange and wondrous land. Among those who lived there was a boy who kept a raven as a pet. He had found the bird with a wounded leg and taken it home and nursed it until it grew well again. But the poor thing was lame.

Tineboy was the youth's name; and the bird was called Mr. Daw. As you may imagine, the raven loved the boy and never left him. There was a cage for it in his bedroom, and there the bird went every night to roost when the sun went down. Birds go to bed quite regularly of their own accord; and if you wished to punish a bird you would make him get up. Birds are not like boys and girls. Just fancy punishing boys or girls by not letting them go to bed at sunset, or by preventing them getting up very early in the morning.

Well, when morning came this bird would get up and stretch himself, and wink his eyes, and give a good shake all over, and then feel quite awake and ready to begin the day.

A bird has a much easier time of it in getting up than a boy or a girl. Soap cannot get into its eye; or the comb will not stick in knots of hair, and its shoe-laces never get into black knots. This is because it does not use soap, or combs, or shoe-laces; if it did, perhaps it also would suffer.

When Mr. Daw had quite finished his own dressing, he would hop on the bed and try and wake his master and make him get up; but of the two, to wake him was the easier task. When the boy went to school the bird would fly along the road beside him, and would sit near on a tree till school was over, and then would follow him home again in the same way.

Tineboy was very fond of Mr. Daw and he used sometimes to try to make him come into the school-room during school-hours. But the bird was very wise, and would not.

One day Tineboy was at his sums, and instead of attending to what he was doing, he kept trying to make Mr. Daw come in. The sum was 'multiply 117,649 by 7.' Tineboy and Mr. Daw kept looking at one another. Tineboy made signals to the bird to come in. Mr. Daw, however, would not stir; he sat outside in the shade, for the day was very hot, and put his head on one side and looked in knowingly.

'Come in, Mr. Daw,' said Tineboy, 'and help me to do this sum.' Mr. Daw only croaked.

'Seven times nine are seventy-seven, seven times nine are seventy-nine – no ninety-seven. Oh, I don't know – I wish number 7 had never been invented,' said Tineboy.

'Croak,' said Mr. Daw.

The day was very hot and Tineboy was very sleepy. He thought that perhaps he would be able to do the sum better if he rested a little while, just to think; and so he put his head down on the table. He was not quite comfortable, for his forehead was on the 7, at least he thought it was; so he shifted it till it hung right down over the edge of the desk. Then, after a while, somehow very queer things began to happen.

The Teacher was just going to tell them a story.

The scholars had all settled themselves down to listen; the Raven sat on the sill of the open window, put his head on one side, closed one eye – the eye nearest the school-room – so that they might think him asleep, and listened away harder than any of them.

The pupils were all happy – all except three. One because his leg went to sleep; another because she had in her pocket some sweets and wanted to eat them, and couldn't without being found out, and the sweets were melting away; and the third, who was awfully sleepy, and awfully anxious to hear the story, and couldn't do either because of the other.

The schoolmaster then began his story which he called 'The Alphabet Doctor.'

At once he was interrupted by Tineboy, who said –

'*What is an Alphabet Doctor?*'

'An Alphabet Doctor,' said the schoolmaster, 'is the doctor who attends to the sicknesses and diseases of the letters of the Alphabet.'

'*How have Alphabets diseases and sicknesses?*' asked Tineboy.

'Oh, they have plenty. Do you never make a crooked o or a capital A with a lame leg, or a T that is not straight in its back?'

There was a chorus from all the class, 'He does. He does often.' Ruffin, the biggest boy, said after all the others, 'Very often. In fact always.'

'Very well, then there must be some one to put them straight again, must there not?'

None of the children could say that there was not. Tineboy alone was heard to mutter to himself, '*I don't believe it.*'

The schoolmaster began again –

'The Alphabet Doctor was sitting down to his tea. He was very tired, for he had been out attending cases all day.'

Tineboy again interrupted, '*What cases?*'

'I can tell you. He had to put in an i which had

been omitted, and to alter the leg of an R which had been twisted into a B.

'Well, just as he was beginning his tea a hurried knock came to the door. He went to the door, opened it, and a groom rushed into the room, breathless with running, and said –

' "Oh, Doctor, do come quick; there is a frightful calamity down at our place."

' "What is our place?" said the doctor.

' "Oh, you know. The Number Stables." '

'*What are the Number Stables?*' said Tineboy, again interrupting.

'The Number Stables,' said the Teacher, 'are the stables where the numbers are kept.'

'*Why are they kept in stables?*' said Tineboy.

'Because they go so fast.'

'*How do they go fast?*'

'You take a sum and work it and you will see at once. Or look at your multiplication table; it starts with twice one are two, and before you get down the page you are at twelve times twelve. Is that not fast going?

'Well, they have to keep the numbers in stables, or else they would run away altogether and never be heard of again. At the end of the day they all come home and change their shoes, and get tied up and have their supper.

'The Groom from the Number Stables was very impatient.

' "What is wrong?" said the Doctor.

' "Oh, poor 7, sir." '

' "What of him?"

' "He is bad. We don't think he'll ever get through it."

' "Through what?" said the Doctor.

' "Come and see," said the Groom.

'The Doctor hurried away, taking the lantern with him, for the night was dark, and soon got to the Stables.

'As he got close there was a very curious sound heard – a sound of gasping and choking, and yelling and coughing, and laughing, and a wild, unearthly screech all in one.

' "Oh, do come quick!" said the Groom.

'When the Doctor entered the stables there was poor No. 7 with all the neighbours round him, and he was in a very bad way. He was foaming at the mouth and apparently quite mad. The Nurse from the Grammar Village was holding him by the hand, trying to bleed him. All the neighbours were wringing either their hands or their necks, or were helping to hold him. The Foot-smith – the man,' explained the teacher, seeing from the look on Tineboy's face that he was going to ask a question, 'the man who puts the feet on the letters and numbers to make them able to stand upright without wearing out – was holding down the poor demented number.

'The Nurse, trying to quiet him, said:

' "There now, there now, deary – don't go and make a noise. Here comes the good Alphabet Doctor, who will make you unmad."

' "I won't be made unmad," said 7, loudly.

' "But, my good sir," said the Doctor, "this cannot go on. You surely are not mad enough to insist on being mad?"

' "Yes, I am," said 7, loudly.

' "Then," said the Doctor blandly, "if you are mad enough to insist on being mad, we must try to cure your madness or being mad, and then you will be unmad enough to wish to be unmad, and we will cure that too." '

'*I don't understand that,*' said Tineboy.

'Hush!' said the class.

'The Doctor took out his stethoscope, and his telescope, and his microscope, and his horoscope, and began to use them on poor mad 7.

'First he put the stethoscope to the sole of his foot, and began to talk into it.

' "That is not the way to use that," said the Nurse; "you ought to put it to his chest and listen to it."

' "Not at all, my dear madam," said the bland Doctor, "that is the way with sane people; but, of course, when one is insane, the fact of the disease necessitates an opposite method of treatment." Then he took the telescope and looked at him to see how near he was, and the microscope to look how small; and then he drew his horoscope.'

'*Why did he draw it?*' said Tineboy.

'Because, my dear child,' said the Teacher, 'do you not see that by right a horoscope is cast; but as the poor man was mad the horoscope had to be drawn.'

'*What is a horrorscope?*' said Tineboy.

'It is not horrorscope, my child; it is horoscope – a very different thing.'

'*Well, what is horoscope?*'

'Look in your dictionary, my dear child,' said the Teacher.

'Well, when the doctor had used all the instruments, he said, "I use all these in order to find the scope of the disease. I shall now proceed to find the cause. In the first instance, I shall interrogate the patient."

' "Now, my good sir, why do you insist on being mad?"

' "Because I choose."

' "Oh, my dear sir, that is not a polite answer. Why do you choose?"

' "I can't say why," said 7, 'unless I make a speech.'

' "Well, make a speech."

' "I can't speak till I am set free; how can I make a speech with all these people holding me?"

' "We are afraid to let you go," said the Nurse, 'you will run away.'

' "I will not."

' "You promise that?" said the doctor.

' "I promise," said 7.

' "Let him go," said the Doctor, and accordingly they put a piece of carpet under him, and the Footsmith sat on his head, the way they do when horses fall down in the street. Then they all got clear away, and the Footsmith got away too; and after a long struggle 7 got to his feet.

' "Now make the speech," said the Doctor.

' "I can't begin," said 7, 'till I get a glass of water on a table. Who ever heard of any one making a speech without a glass of water!'

'So they brought a glass of water.

' "Ladies and Gentlemen –" began 7, and then stopped.

' "What are you waiting for?" said the Doctor.

' "For the applause, of course," said 7. "Who ever heard of a speech without applause?"

'They all applauded.

' "I am mad," said 7, 'because I choose to be mad; and I never shall, will, might, could, should, would, or ought to be anything but mad. The treatment that I get is enough to make me mad.'

' "Dear me, dear me!" said the Doctor. 'What treatment?'

' "Morning, noon, and night am I treated worse than any slave. There is not in the whole range of learning any one thing that has so much to bear as I have. I work hard all the time. I never grumble. I am often a multiple; often a multiplicated. I am willing to bear my share of being a result, but I cannot stand the treatment I get. I am wrong added, wrong divided, wrong subtracted, and wrong multiplied. Other numbers are not treated as I am; and, besides, they are not orphans like me."

' "Orphans?" asked the Doctor; 'what do you mean?'

' "I mean that the other numbers have lots of relations. But I have neither kith nor kin – except old

Number I, and he does not count for much; and, besides, I am only his great-great-great-great-grandson."

' "How do you mean?" asked the Doctor.

' "Oh, he is an old chap that is there all the time. He has all his children round him, and I only come six generations down."

' "Humph!" said the doctor.

' "Number 2," went on 7, "never gets into any trouble, and 4, 6, and 8 are his cousins. Number 3 is close to 6 and 9. No. 5 is half a decimal and he never gets into trouble. But as for me, I am miserable, ill-treated, and alone." Here poor 7 began to cry, and bending down his head sobbed bitterly.'

When the Teacher got thus far there was an interruption, for here little Tineboy began to cry too.

'Why are you crying?' said Ruffin, the bully boy.

'*I am not crying,*' said Tineboy, and he cried away faster than ever.

The Teacher went on with the story.

'The Alphabet Doctor tried to cheer poor 7.

' "Hear, hear!" said he.

'7 stopped crying and looked at him. "No," said he, 'you should say "speak, speak," it is I that should say "hear, hear." '

' "Certainly," said the Doctor, 'you would say that if you were sane; but then, you see, you are not sane, and being mad you say what you should not say.'

' "That is false," said 7.

' "I understand," said the Doctor, 'but do not stop

to argue the point. If you were sane you would say "that is true," but you do say "that is false," meaning that you agree with me.'

'7 looked pleased at being so understood.

' "No," said he – meaning 'yes.'

' "Then," continued the Doctor, 'if you say "speak, speak," when a sane man would say "hear, hear," of course, I should say 'hear, hear,' when I mean 'speak, speak,' because I am talking to a madman.'

' "No, no," said 7 – meaning, 'yes, yes.'

' "Go on with your speech," said the Doctor.

'No 7 took out his handkerchief and wept.

' "Ladies and Gentlemen," he went on, "once more I must plead the cause of the poor ill-used number – that is me – this orphan number – this number without kin –"'

Here Tineboy interrupted the Teacher, '*How had he no skin?*'

'Kin, my child. Kin, not skin,' said the Teacher.

'*What is the difference between kin and skin?*' asked Tineboy.

'There will be but a small difference,' said the Teacher, 'between this cane and your skin if you interrupt.' So Tineboy was quiet.

'Well,' said the teacher, 'poor 7 went on – "I implore your pity for this forlorn number. Oh, you boys and girls, think of a poor desolate number, who has no home, no friends, no father, mother, brother, sister, uncle, aunt, nephew, niece, son, daughter, or cousin, and is desolate and alone."'

Tineboy here set up a terrible howl.

'What are you crying for?' said the Teacher.

'*I want poor old 7 to be more happy. I will give him some of my lunch and a share of my bed.*'

The Teacher turned to the Monitor.

'Tineboy is a good child,' he said,' let him for the next week learn 7 times 0 up, and perhaps that will comfort him.'

The Raven, sitting in the window, winked his eye to himself and hopped about with a suppressed merry croak, shook his wings, and seemed to be hugging himself and laughing. Then he hopped softly away, and stole up and hid on the top of the book-case.

The Schoolmaster went on with his story.

'Well, children, after a while poor 7 got better and promised that he would get unmad. Before the Doctor went home again all the Alphabet and Number Children came and shook poor Number 7's hand, and promised that they would be more kind to him in future.

'Now, children, what do you think of the story?'

They all said that they liked it, that it was beautiful, and that they too would try to be more kind to poor 7 in the future. At last Ruffin the bully boy said:

'I don't believe it. And if it is true I wish he had died; we would be better without him.'

'Would we?' asked the teacher, 'how?'

'Because we would not be troubled with him,' said Ruffin.

As he said it there was a sort of queer croak heard from the Raven, but nobody minded, except Tineboy, who said:

'*Mr. Daw, you and I love poor 7, at all events.*'

The Raven hated Ruffin because he always threw stones at him, and he had tried to pull the feathers out of his tail, and when Ruffin spoke, his croak seemed to mean, 'Just you wait.' When no one was looking Mr. Daw stole up and hid in the rafters.

Then presently school broke up, and Tineboy went home; but he was not able to find Mr. Daw. He thought he was lost, and was very miserable, and went to bed crying.

In the meantime, when the school was locked up and empty, Mr. Daw came down from the rafters very, very quietly – hobbled over to the door, and putting his head down, listened; then he flew and scrambled up on the handle of the door, and looked out through the keyhole. There was nothing to see and nothing to hear.

Then he got up on the Master's desk, flapped his wings, and began to crow like a cock, only very softly, for fear he should be heard.

Presently he went over all the room, flying up to the big sheets of multiplication table, and turning over the pages of the books with his claws, and picking up SOMETHING with his sharp beak.

One would hardly believe it, but he was stealing all the Number Sevens in the place; he picked the Seven off the clock, rubbed it off the slates, and brushed it with his wings off the blackboard.

Mr. Daw knew that if once you can get the whole of any number out of a schoolroom no one else can use it without asking your leave.

Whilst he was picking out all the Sevens he was swelling out very much; and when he had got them all he was exactly Seven times his natural size.

He was not able to do this all at once. It took him the whole night, and when he got back to his corner in the rafters it was nearly time for school to open.

He was now so big that he was only just able to squeeze into the corner and no more.

The school time came, but there was no Master, and there were no Scholars. A whole hour passed; and then the Master came with the boys and girls.

When they were all in, the Master said –

'You are all very late.'

'Please, sir, we could not help it,' they all answered together.

'Why could you not help it?'

They all answered at once –

'I wasn't called in time.'

'What time are you called at every morning?'

They all seemed about to speak, but all were silent.

'Why don't you answer?' asked the Teacher.

They made motions with their mouths like speaking, but no one said anything.

The Raven up in his corner croaked a quiet laugh all to himself.

'Why don't you answer?' asked the Teacher again. 'If I do not have my question answered at once, I shall keep you all in.'

'Please, sir, we can't,' said one.

'Why not?'

'Because' –

Here Tineboy interrupted, '*Why were you so late, sir?*'

'Well, my boy, I am sorry to say I was late; but the fact is, my servant did not knock at my door at the usual hour.'

'*What hour, sir?*' asked Tineboy.

The Teacher seemed as if he was going to speak, but stopped.

'This is very queer,' he said, after a long pause.

Ruffin said, in a sort of swaggering way, 'We are not late at all. You are here and we are here – that is all.'

'No, it is not all,' said the Teacher. 'Ten is the hour, and it is now eleven – we have lost an hour.'

'How have we lost it?' asked one of the Scholars.

'Well, that is what puzzles me. We must only wait a little and see.'

Here Tineboy said suddenly, '*Perhaps some one stole it!*'

'Stole what?' said the scholars.

'*I don't know,*' said Tineboy.

They all laughed.

'*You need not laugh, something is stolen; look at my lesson!*' said Tineboy, and he held up the book. Here is what they saw –

–	1	are	–
–	2	„	14
–	3	„	21
–	4	„	28
–	5	„	35

```
–   6   „   42
–   7   „   49
–   8   „   56
–   9   „   63
–  10   „   –0
```

All the Scholars crowded round Tineboy to look at the book. Ruffin did not, for he was looking at the school clock.

'The clock has lost something,' said he, and sure enough it did not look at all right.

The Teacher looked up – for he was leaning with his head on his desk, groaning.

'What is wrong with it?' he asked.

'Something is missing.'

'There is a number out; there are only eleven figures,' said the Teacher.

'No, no,' said the Scholars.

'Count them out, Ruffin,' said the Master.

'1 2 3 4 5 6 8 9 10 11 12.'

'Quite right,' said the Teacher, 'you see there are twelve. No there are not – yes there are – no – yes – no, yes – what is it all about?' and he looked round the room, and then leaned his head on the desk again and groaned.

In the meantime the Raven had crept along the rafters till he had got over the Teacher's desk; and then he got a good heavy Seven and dropped it right on the little bald spot on the top of the Teacher's head. It bounded off the head and fell on the desk before him. The instant the Teacher saw it he knew what was missing all the time. He covered over the

Seven with a piece of blotting paper. He then called up Ruffin.

'Ruffin, you told me that something was missing – are you sure?'

'Yes, of course.'

'Very well. Do you remember that you said yesterday, that you wished a certain Number had died in a madhouse?'

'Yes, I do; and I wish it still.'

'Well, that Number has been stolen by some one during the night.'

'Hurrah!' said Ruffin, and he threw his book up to the ceiling. It hit poor Mr. Daw, who had another Seven in his beak ready to drop it, and knocked the Seven down. It fell into Tineboy's cap, which he held in his hand. He took it out, and stooped and petted it.

'*Poor 7*,' said Tineboy.

'Give me the Number,' said Ruffin.

'*I shan't. It belongs to me.*'

'Then I'll make you,' said Ruffin; and he caught hold of Tineboy – even before the Master's face.

'*Let me go. I'll not give you my poor Seven,*' said Tineboy, and he began to scream and cry.

'Ruffin, stand out,' said the Master.

Ruffin did so.

'Seven times seven?' asked the Master.

Ruffin did not answer. He could not, for he had not got a Seven.

'*I know,*' said Tineboy.

'Oh, yes,' said Ruffin, with a sneer; 'he knows because he has a Number.'

'*Forty-nine,*' said Tineboy.

'Right,' said the Master; 'go up, Tineboy.'

So Tineboy went up to the top of the class, and Ruffin went down.

'Seven times forty-nine?' asked the Master.

They were all silent.

'Come, answer!' said the Master.

'*What is it, yourself?*' said Tineboy.

'Well, my boy, I am sorry to say I cannot say. Dear me, it is very queer,' and the Master put down his head on the desk again, and groaned louder than ever.

Just then Mr. Daw took another seven and dropped it down on the floor before Tineboy.

'Three hundred and forty-three,' said Tineboy, quickly; for he could answer as he had another Seven.

The Teacher looked up and laughed loudly.

'Hurrah, hurrah!' said he.

When the third Seven fell the Raven began to swell.

He got seven times as big as he was, so that he began to lift the slates off the roof.

The Scholars all looked up; Ruffin had his mouth open, and Mr. Daw, anxious to get rid of the Sevens, dropped one into it.

'Two thousand three hundred and one,' Ruffin spluttered out.

Mr. Daw dropped another Seven into his mouth,

and he spluttered out again worse than ever, 'Sixteen thousand eight hundred and seven.'

The Raven began hurling Sevens at him as fast as he could; and each time he threw one he grew smaller and smaller, till he got to just his natural size.

Ruffin kept spluttering out and gasping numbers as hard as ever he could, till he grew black in the face and fell down in a fit just as he had come to 'Seventy-nine thousand seven hundred and ninety-two billion, two hundred and sixty-six thousand two hundred and ninety-seven million six hundred and twelve thousand and one.'

Suddenly Tineboy woke up, and found that he had been dreaming with his head down.

*   *   *

BRAM STOKER was the author of *Dracula*, the scariest horror story of all. His tale of the vampire count from Transylvania has been read by millions of people all over the world ever since it was first published just over a century ago in 1897. It has also inspired many writers of spooky stories – including most of those in this book – and been made into countless films, notably those starring Bela Lugosi and Christopher Lee. Although *Dracula* remains the best known of his books, Bram Stoker also wrote several other really frightening tales, including *The Jewel of the Seven Stars* (1907) in which an ancient Egyptian queen attempts to resurrect herself after lying in a tomb for 5,000 years; *The Lady of the Shroud*

(1909) about a princess who poses as an evil, blood-sucking vampire; and *The Lair of the White Worm* (1911) in which a monstrous worm hidden for thousands of years in a bottomless well re-emerges as a beautiful, alluring woman.

For much of his life, Abraham (Bram) Stoker worked as a theatrical manager for the famous Victorian actor and impresario, Sir Henry Irving. Yet ever since his childhood in Ireland he had been writing stories and his first book was a collection of fantasies for younger readers, *Under The Sunset*, published in 1882, copies of which are now very rare indeed. Several of the tales were based on Irish legends that his mother had told him, including 'The Spectre of Doom', inspired by a cholera plague that had swept across the country killing thousands of men, women and children. 'How 7 Went Mad' also appeared in the collection and is reprinted in this book for the first time in many years.

KITTENS

Dean Koontz

Marnie is waiting patiently for the family cat, Pinkie, to have a new litter of kittens. She had four last year, but the trouble was that they just disappeared a few days after they were born. Marnie's dad told her it had been, 'the will of God' and that the kittens were now in Heaven. But he wouldn't explain what had happened to them. Since then, her mum has given birth to twins and both babies are thriving. Surely this year the same thing won't happen to the kittens? So when Pinkie safely gives birth to six kittens out in the barn, Marnie vows to keep an eye on them every minute of the day. She hides out behind a pile of straw and when the tragedy looks likely to be repeated, Marnie gets a very scary idea indeed for revenge . . .

*   *   *

The cool green water slipped along the streambed, bubbling around smooth brown stones, reflecting the melancholy willows that lined the bank. Marnie sat on the grass, tossing stones into a deep pool, watching ripples spread in ever-widening circles and lap at the muddy banks. She was thinking about the kittens. This year's kittens, not last year's. A year ago, her parents had told her that the kittens had gone to

Heaven. Pinkie's litter had disappeared the third day after their squealing birth.

Marnie's father had said, 'God took them away to Heaven to live with Him.'

She didn't exactly doubt her father. After all, he was a religious man. He taught Sunday school every week and was an officer or something in the church, whose duty it was to count collection money and mark it down in a little red book. He was always picked to give the sermon on Laymen's Sunday. And every evening, he read passages to them from the Bible. She had been late for the reading last night and had been spanked. 'Spare the rod and spoil the child,' her father always said. No, she didn't actually doubt her father, for if anyone would know about God and kittens, it was he.

But she continued to wonder. Why, when there were hundreds upon thousands of kittens in the world, did God have to take all four of hers? Was God selfish?

This was the first that she had thought of those kittens for some time. In the past twelve months, much had happened to make her forget. There was her first year in school, the furor of getting ready for the first day – the buying of paper, pencils, and books. And the first few weeks had been interesting, meeting Mr Alphabet and Mr Numbers. When school began to bore her, Christmas rushed in on polished runners and glistening ice: the shopping, the green and yellow and red and blue lights, the Santa Claus on the corner who staggered when he walked, the candlelit church on Christmas Eve when she had had to go to the bathroom and her father had made her wait until the service was over. When things began to lose momentum again in March, her mother had given birth to twins. Marnie had been surprised at how small they were and at how slowly they seemed to grow in the following weeks.

Here it was June again. The twins were three months old, finally beginning to grow a great deal heavier; school was out, and Christmas was an eternity away, and everything was getting dull again. Therefore, when she heard her father telling her mother that Pinkie was going to have another litter, she grasped at the news and wrenched every drop of excitement from it. She busied herself in the kitchen, preparing rags and cotton for the birth and a fancy box for the kittens' home when they arrived.

As events ran their natural course, Pinkie slunk away and had the kittens during the night in a dark corner of the barn. There was no need for sterilized rags or cotton, but the box came in handy. There were six in this litter, all gray with black spots that looked like ink hastily blotted.

She liked the kittens, and she was worried about them. What if God was watching again like last year?

'What are you doing, Marnie?'

She didn't have to look; she knew who was behind her. She turned anyway, out of deference, and saw her father glaring down at her, dark irregular splotches of perspiration discoloring the underarms of his faded blue work coveralls, dirt smeared on his chin and caked to the beard on his left cheek.

'Throwing stones,' she answered quietly.

'At the fish?'

'Oh, no, sir. Just throwing stones.'

'Do we remember who was the victim of stone throwing?' He smiled a patronizing smile.

'Saint Stephen,' she answered.

'Very good.' The smile faded. 'Supper's ready.'

She sat ramrod stiff in the old maroon easy chair, looking attentive as her father read to them from the ancient family Bible that was bound in black leather, all scuffed and with several torn pages. Her mother sat next to her father on the dark-blue corduroy couch, hands folded in her lap, an isn't-it-wonderful-what-God-has-given-us smile painted on her plain but pretty face.

'Suffer the little children to come to Me, and forbid them not; for such is the Kingdom of God.' Her father closed the book with a gentle slap that seemed to leap into the stale air and hang there, holding up a thick curtain of silence. No one spoke for several minutes. Then: 'What chapter of what book did we just read, Marnie?'

'Saint Mark, chapter ten,' she said dutifully.

'Fine,' he said. Turning to his wife, whose smile had changed to a we've-done-what-a-Christian-family-should-do expression, he said, 'Mary, how about coffee for us and a glass of milk for Marnie?'

'Right,' said her mother, getting up and pacing into the kitchen.

Her father sat there, examining the inside covers of the old holy book, running his fingers along the cracks in the yellow paper, scrutinizing the ghostly stains embedded forever in the title page where some great-uncle had accidentally spilled wine a million-billion years ago.

'Father,' she said tentatively.

He looked up from the book, not smiling, not frowning.

'What about the kittens?'

'What about them?' he countered.

'Will God take them again this year?'

The half-smile that had crept onto his face evaporated into the thick air of the living room. 'Perhaps,' was all that he said.

'He can't,' she almost sobbed.

'Are you saying what God can and cannot do, young lady?'

'No, sir.'

'God can do anything.'

'Yes, sir.' She fidgeted in her chair, pushing herself deeper into its rough, worn folds. 'But why would He want my kittens again? Why always mine?'

'I've had quite enough of this, Marnie. Now be quiet.'

'But why mine?' she persisted.

He stood suddenly, crossed to the chair, and slapped her delicate face. A thin trickle of blood slipped from the corner of her mouth. She wiped it away with the palm of her hand.

'You must not doubt God's motives!' her father

insisted. 'You are far too young to doubt.' The saliva glistened on his lips. He grabbed her by the arm and brought her to her feet. 'Now you get up those stairs and into bed.'

She didn't argue. On the way to the staircase, she wiped away the re-forming stream of blood. She walked slowly up the steps, allowing her hand to run along the smooth, polished wood railing.

'Here's the milk,' she heard her mother saying below.

'We won't be needing it,' her father answered curtly.

In her room, she lay in the semidarkness that came when the full moon shone through her window, its orange-yellow light glinting from a row of religious plaques that lined one wall. In her parents' room, her mother was cooing to the twins, changing their diapers. 'God's little angels,' she heard her mother say. Her father was tickling them, and she could hear the 'angels' chuckling – a deep gurgle that rippled from down in their fat throats.

Neither her father nor her mother came to say good night. She was being punished.

Marnie was sitting in the barn, petting one of the gray kittens, postponing an errand her mother had sent her on ten minutes earlier. The rich smell of dry, golden hay filled the air. Straw covered the floor and crackled underfoot. In the far end of the building, the cows were lowing to each other – only two of them, whose legs had been sliced by barbed wire and who were being made to convalesce. The kitten mewed and pawed the air below her chin.

'Where's Marnie?' her father's voice boomed from somewhere in the yard between the house and the barn.

She was about to answer when she heard her mother call from the house: 'I sent her to Brown's for a recipe of Helen's. She'll be gone another twenty minutes.'

'That's plenty of time,' her father answered. The crunch of his heavy shoes on the cinder path echoed in military rhythm.

Marnie knew that something was wrong; something was happening that she was not supposed to see. Quickly, she put the kitten back in the red and gold box and sprawled behind a pile of straw to watch.

Her father entered, drew a bucket of water from the wall tap, and placed it in front of the kittens. Pinkie hissed and arched her back. The man picked her up and shut her in an empty oat bin from which her anguished squeals boomed in a ridiculously loud echo that belonged on the African veldt and not on an American farm. Marnie almost laughed, but remembered her father and suppressed the levity.

He turned again to the box of kittens. Carefully, he lifted one by the scruff of the neck, petted it twice, and thrust its head under the water in the bucket! There was a violent thrashing from within the bucket, and sparkling droplets of water sprayed into the air. Her father grimaced and shoved the entire body under the smothering pool. In time, the thrashing ceased. Marnie found that her fingers were digging into the concrete floor, hurting her.

Why? Why-why-why?

Her father lifted the limp body from the bucket. Something pink and bloody hung from the animal's mouth. She couldn't tell whether it was the tongue or whether the precious thing had spewed its entrails into the water in a last attempt to escape the heavy, horrible death of suffocation.

Soon six kittens were dead. Soon six silent fur balls were dropped in a burlap sack. The top was twisted shut. He let Pinkie out of the bin. The shivering cat followed him out of the barn, mewing softly, hissing when he turned to look at her.

Marnie lay very still for a long time, thinking of nothing but the execution and trying desperately to understand. Had God sent her father? Was it God who told him to kill the kittens – to take them away from her? If it was, she didn't see how she could ever again stand before that gold and white altar, accepting communion. She stood and walked toward the house, blood dripping from her fingers, blood and cement.

'Did you get the recipe?' asked her mother as Marnie slammed the kitchen door.

'Mrs Brown couldn't find it. She'll send it over tomorrow.' She lied so well that she surprised herself. 'Did God take my kittens?' she blurted suddenly.

Her mother looked confused. 'Yes,' was all that she could say.

'I'll get even with God! He can't do that! He can't!' She ran out of the kitchen toward the staircase.

Her mother watched but didn't try to stop her.

Marnie Caufield walked slowly up the stairs, letting her hand run along the smooth, polished wood railing.

At noon, when Walter Caufield came in from the field, he heard a loud crash and the tinkling of china and the shattering of glass. He rushed into the living room to see his wife lying at the foot of the stairs. A novelty table was overturned, statuettes broken and cracked.

'Mary, Mary. Are you hurt?' He bent quickly to her side.

She looked up at him out of eyes that were far away in distant mists. 'Walt! My Good God, Walt – our precious angels. The bathtub – our precious angels!'

*   *   *

DEAN KOONTZ is one of the biggest selling authors of horror fiction in the world today with sales that almost match that other great American writer of spooky fiction, Stephen King. He grew up in a very poor family with a father who treated him extremely badly. Dean Koontz' one escape was in to books – especially fantasy stories and he recalls vividly 'shivering at *Frankenstein* and cringing from *Dracula*'. He began to pursue his ambition of becoming a writer while still at Bedford High School in Pennsylvania and his very first story to be published was the one you have just read. He explains, ' "Kittens" was written while I was in college, won a prize in an annual fiction competition for college students sponsored by the *Atlantic Monthly* and then earned me fifty dollars when it was bought by a magazine called *Readers & Writers*. As I recall, *Readers & Writers* went belly up soon thereafter!'

After Dean Koontz had left college and worked for several years as a teacher, his wife made him an offer he says he could not refuse. She would support him for five years and if he had not become a successful writer in that time, then he should return to teaching. After producing a string of crime and mystery novels under his own name and several pseudonyms, he won international fame with a series of single word titles including *Chase* (1972), *Strangers* (1986) and *Lightning* (1988) and he never needed to contemplate returning to the classroom again. He has, though, continued to interest himself in young readers and their likes and dislikes. Dean Koontz has also drawn on his own unhappy childhood for some of his most memorable novels and stories in the same tradition as 'Kittens'.

HORROR SNAP

Pete Johnson

Amy's Polaroid camera takes pretty gross photographs. Especially of other kids, like her best friend, Karen, who took one look at a picture of her and screamed, 'This isn't me – it's a red-eyed mutant having a bad hair day!' Pretty soon everyone who knew Amy was running away from what they called her 'demon camera'. The thing was, she had actually bought the camera at a car-boot sale so she really has no idea where it had come from. So, when she finally gets bored of taking the unflattering photographs, Amy just leaves the camera in her bedroom. Then, one night, she wakes up to find something very scary happening. The camera is now busy whirring and flashing on its own . . .

*   *   *

It all began when I bought a camera at a car-boot sale. Next day I got a film, then started snapping all my friends. It was a Polaroid, so as soon as you pressed the button, there would be a great flash of light, a whirring noise, and the camera would spit the picture out at you.

Karen, my best friend, snatched my photo of her.

'Amy, this isn't me,' she cried. 'This is a red-eyed mutant having a bad hair day.'

None of my pictures were very flattering, so it

wasn't surprising my friends were soon fleeing from me and my 'demon camera', as they called it. Everyone, that is, except my two little brothers, Ryan who's two, and Niall, who's four.

Soon I got bored of my camera. It sat on my dressing table looking sad and neglected. Then one night, I woke up with a start. I had the strangest feeling someone had just shone a bright torch in my face.

'Who's there?' I whispered, hoping I sounded braver than I felt.

Someone answered. Only it wasn't a human's voice I heard. It was my camera whirring away in the darkness.

But that was impossible. My camera couldn't just switch itself on. I reached out to put on my bedside light. At once, the camera stopped. My room was silent once more.

Very slowly, I scrambled out of bed. I approached the camera as if it were an unexploded bomb. I half expected it to start whirring again. And then I noticed there was something waiting for me in the camera. A photograph.

I pulled it out. A picture was starting to form. It was very blurry, but I could just make out Ryan's face. His eyes were wide and staring and his hair looked to be dripping wet . . . and someone was holding onto him. It was me. I recognised one of my rings. What a nasty, horrible photo. I let out a cry and my mum heard me. She came racing in.

'Whatever's the matter?'

'Look,' I cried, waving the snap at her. But the image had vanished. I tried to explain what had happened.

'Sometimes we can think we're awake when we are still half asleep,' she said.

Mum decided I'd been over-working at school and said it was just as well half term was coming up. At times I convinced myself it had been just a 'nasty dream'. But there was still the evidence of the phantom snap.

I moved my camera into the bottom of my wardrobe and tried to forget about it. Karen was away for half term so I spent most of the week lying in the May sunshine, reading and refereeing the many arguments between my two little brothers. Mum did her best to keep them entertained. She even set up the garden slide so that it led into the paddling pool. But nothing seemed to please them for long.

Then it was Friday afternoon. Mum popped next door for 'ten minutes', because Mr Serling had just come back from having a hip operation. I promised to keep an eye on the boys.

The doorbell rang. Niall and Ryan charged to the front door. I pushed past them.

'I'm in charge,' I said.

To my great surprise, Karen was standing there.

'You're not back until tomorrow,' I exclaimed.

'Oh you won't believe what's happened,' she said. 'We've just had the holiday from hell.' She started to tell me about it. Karen soon had me laughing.

Then I looked around me.

'Where have Ryan and Niall gone?'

'They ran off,' said Karen. 'They'll be playing somewhere – or they could be hiding.'

'We'd better go and look for them.'

'Just let me finish my story first,' Karen began talking again.

But I didn't hear her. That photograph of Ryan I'd seen suddenly flashed through my head. A great shiver ran through me. All at once I knew where Ryan was.

Without a word to Karen, I tore out into the garden. Ryan was lying face down in the paddling pool. I sprang forward and picked him up. Water was dripping all down his face. His eyes were wide and staring. He wasn't breathing.

Immediately I blew into Ryan's mouth. I felt him gasp. His eyes moved. Then he started to cry. I clasped him tightly, whispering 'Everything's going to be alright.'.

Watching all this from the top of the garden, was Niall. He was standing very still. When I called out his name, he put his hands over his face and started to shake.

Later he confessed what had happened. Ryan had dared to climb the slide steps in front of him. So, just as Ryan got to the top, Niall pushed him face first into the paddling pool. Then he got scared and hid.

Niall was kissing Ryan now and saying 'Sorry, sorry,' over and over. Ryan still looked a little bit stunned. But he was starting to enjoy the attention, too.

'If you hadn't rushed out to the garden when you did . . .' began Karen. She stared at me. 'But how did you know?'

I just shrugged my shoulders. How could I tell her it was my camera that knew – and had warned me?

I was very grateful to it. Yet I was scared, too. Scared that one night soon, I would hear a whirring noise and there, waiting for me, would be another terrifying glimpse into the future.

*   *   *

PETE JOHNSON is another teacher turned writer whose books have earned rave reviews and won awards. His nightmare tale of a bloodthirsty, howling monster, *The Ghost Dog*, won the *Young Telegraph* Fully Booked Award and the Stockton Libraries Children's Book of the Year in 1997, a feat he repeated in 2001 with *The Creeper*. The success of his other books such as *My Friend's A Werewolf* (1997) and *The Phantom Thief* (1998) can also be attributed to the care he takes in visiting lots of schools and libraries – even in Europe where his books are translated – to keep in touch with his readers. Pete Johnson receives over a hundred letters a month from teenagers wanting to join his panel of readers in a collaboration which helps him to give a sense of intimacy amidst all the horrors. He says, 'One of the best things an author can do is show the reader that he, or she, is not on their own.'

Born in Winchester, Pete Johnson went to Birmingham University and had a number of jobs before teaching English and Drama at a secondary school in Buckinghamshire. There he wrote his first novel, *Secrets From The School Underground* (1990) based on his observations of his students. This was an immediate hit and allowed him to become a full-time author. He sees his writing as 'an incredible form of investigation' and has been on ghost hunts while researching several titles, notably *The Dead Hour* (1993). Pete Johnson likes collecting old computers – he recently had an exhibit at the Vintage Computer Festival – and photography. He explains: 'I have some completely unorganised, very large and sometimes blurry pictures from my digital camera. Mostly they are pictures taken in our community . . .' Was it these photographs that inspired 'Horror Snap' perhaps?

WHEN WE WENT TO SEE THE END OF THE WORLD BY DAWNIE MORNINGSIDE, AGE 11¼

Neil Gaiman

It's a special holiday weekend and Dawnie wants to go pony riding. But her dad has other ideas. The whole family is going to see what he calls, 'the end of the world'. When Dawnie's mum argues, Dad says it is time his daughter got some idea of what was going on with people. So, complete with a picnic, Dawnie, her baby sister, Daisy, and Mum and Dad set off in their car. As they drive, night falls and outside, Dawnie sees everything getting stranger – especially after they are sent a different way by a DIVERSION sign. But none of this is quite so scary as what lies in wait for Dawnie and her family on the other side of the hill where Dad says the end of the world lies . . .

*   *   *

What I did on the founders day holiday was, my dad said we were going to have a picnic, and my mum said where, and I said I wanted to go to Ponydale and ride the ponies, but my dad said we were going to the end of the world and my mum said oh god and my dad said now, Tanya, its time the child got to see what was what and my mum said no, no, she just meant that shed thought that Johnsons Peculiar Garden of Lights was nice this time of year.

My mum loves Johnsons Peculiar Garden of Lights, which is in Lux, between 12th street and the river, and I like it too, especially when they give you potato sticks and you feed them to the little white chipmunks who come all the way up to the picnic table.

This is the word for the white chipmunks. Albino.

Dolorita Hunsickle says that the chipmunks tell your fortune if you catch them but I never did. She says a chipmunk told her she would grow up to be a famous ballerina and that she would die of consumption unloved in a boardinghouse in Prague.

So my dad made potato salad.

Here is the recipe.

My dads potato salad is made with tiny new potatoes, which he boils, then while they're warm he pours his secret mix over them which is mayonnaise and sour cream and little onion things called chives which he sotays in bacon fat, and crunchy bacon bits. When it gets cool its the best potato salad in the world, and better than the potato salad we get at school which tastes like white sick.

We stopped at the shop and got fruit and Cocacola and potato sticks, and they went into the box and it went into the back of the car and we went into the car and mum and dad and my baby sister. We Are On Our Way!

Where our house is, it is morning, when we leave, and we got onto the motorway and we went over the bridge over twilight, and soon it got dark. I love driving through the dark.

I sit in the back of the car and I got all scrunched singing songs that go lah lah lah in the back of my head so my dad has to go, Dawnie darling stop making that noise, but still I go lah lah lah.

Lah lah lah.

The motorway was closed for repairs so we followed signs and this is what they said: DIVERSION.

Mummy made dad lock his door, while we were driving, and she made me to lock my door too.

It got more darker as we went.

This is what I saw while we drived through the centre of the city, out of the window. I saw a beardy man who ran out when we stopped at the lights and ran a smeary cloth all over our windows.

He winked at me through the window, in the back of the car, with his old eyes.

Then he wasnt there any more, and mummy and daddy had an arguement about who he was, and whether he was good luck or bad luck. But not a bad arguement.

There were more signs that said DIVERSION, and they were yellow.

I saw a street where the prettiest men Id ever seen blew us kisses and sung songs, and a street where I saw a woman holding the side of her face under a blue light but her face was bleeding and wet, and a street where there were only cats who stared at us.

My sister went loo loo, which means look and she said kitty.

The baby is called Melicent, but I call her Daisy-daisy. Its my secret name for her. Its from a song called Daisydaisy, which goes, Daisydaisy give me your answer do Im half crazy over the love of you it wont be a stylish marriage I cant afford a carriage but youll look sweet upon the seat of a bicycle made for two.

Then we were out of the city, into the hills.

Then there were houses that were like palaces on each side of the road, set far back.

My dad was born in one of those houses, and he and mummy had the arguement about money where he says what he threw away to be with her and she says oh, so your bringing that up again are you?

I looked at the houses. I asked my Daddy which one Grandmother lived in. He said he didnt know, which he was lying. I dont know why grownups fib so much, like when they say Ill tell you later or well see when they mean no or I wont tell you at all even when your older.

In one house there were people dancing in the garden. Then the road began to wind around, and daddy was driving us through the countryside through the dark.

Look! said my mother. A white deer ran across the road with people chasing it. My dad said they were a nuisance and they were a pest and like rats with antlers, and the worst bit of hitting a deer is when it comes through the glass into the car and he said he had a friend who was kicked to death by a deer who came through the glass with sharp hooves.

And mummy said oh god like we really needed to know that, and daddy said well it happened Tanya, and mummy said honestly your incorigible.

I wanted to ask who the people chasing the deer was, but I started to sing instead going lah lah lah lah lah lah.

My dad said stop that. My mum said for gods sake let the girl express herself, and Dad said I bet you like chewing tinfoil too and my mummy said so whats that supposed to mean and Daddy said nothing and I said arent we there yet?

On the side of the road there were bonfires, and sometimes piles of bones.

We stopped on one side of a hill. The end of the world was on the other side of the hill, said my dad.

I wondered what it looked like. We parked the car in the car park. We got out. Mummy carried Daisy. Daddy carried the picnic basket. We walked over the hill, in the light of the candles they set by the path. A unicorn came up to me on the way. It was white as snow, and it nuzzled me with its mouth.

I asked daddy if I could give it an apple and he said it probably has fleas, and Mummy said it didnt. and all the time its tail went swish swish swish.

I offered it my apple it looked at me with big silver eyes and then it snorted like this, hrrrmph, and ran away over the hill.

Baby Daisy said loo loo.

This is what it looks like at the end of the world, which is the best place in the world.

There is a hole in the ground, which looks like a

very wide big hole and pretty people holding sticks and simatars that burn come up out of it. They have long golden hair. They look like princesses, only fierce. Some of them have wings and some of them dusnt.

And theres a big hole in the sky too and things are coming down from it, like the cat-heady man, and the snakes made out of stuff that looks like glitter-jel like I putted on my hair at Hallowmorn, and I saw something that looked like a big old buzzie fly, coming down from the sky. There were very many of them. As many as stars.

They dont move. They just hang there, not doing anything. I asked Daddy why they weren't moving and he said they were moving just very very slowly but I dont think so.

We set up at a picnic table.

Daddy said the best thing about the end of the world was no wasps and no moskitos. And mummy said there werent a lot of wasps in Johnsons Peculiar Garden of Lights either. I said there werent alot of wasps or moskitos at Ponydale and there were ponies too we could ride on and my Dad said hed brought us here to enjoy ourselves.

I said I wanted to go over to see if I could see the unicorn again and mummy and daddy said dont go too far.

At the next table to us were people with masks on. I went off with Daisydaisy to see them.

They sang Happy Birthday to you to a big fat lady with no clothes on, and a big funny hat. She had lots of bosoms all the way down to her tummy. I waited to see her blow out the candles on her cake, but there wasnt a cake.

Arent you going to make a wish? I said.

She said she couldnt make any more wishes. She was too old. I told her that at my last birthday when I blew out my candles all in one go I had thought about my wish for a long time, and I was going to wish that mummy and Daddy wouldn't argue any more in the night. But in the end I wished for a shetland pony but it never come.

The lady gave me a cuddle and said I was so cute that she could just eat me all up, bones and hair and everything. She smelled like sweet dried milk.

Then Daisydaisy started to cry with all her might and mane, and the lady putted me down.

I shouted and called for the unicorn, but I didnt see him. Sometimes I thought I could hear a trumpet, and sometimes I thought it was just the noise in my ears.

Then we came back to the table. Whats after the end of the world I said to my dad. Nothing he said. Nothing at all. Thats why its called the end.

Then Daisy was sick over Daddys shoes, and we cleaned it up.

I sat by the table. We ate potato salad, which I gave you the recipe for all ready, you should make it its really good, and we drank orange juice and potato sticks and squishy egg and cress sandwiches. We drank our Coca-cola.

Then Mummy said something to Daddy I didnt

hear and he just hit her in the face with a big hit with his hand, and mummy started to cry.

Daddy told me to take Daisy and walk about while they talked.

I took Daisy and I said come on Daisydaisy, come on old daisybell because she was crying too, but Im too old to cry.

I couldnt hear what they were saying. I looked up at the cat face man and I tried to see if he was moving very very slowly, and I heard the trumpet at the end of the world in my head going dah dah dah.

We sat by a rock and I sang songs to Daisy lah lah lah lah lah to the sound of the trumpet in my head dah dah dah.

Lah lah lah lah lah lah lah lah.

Lah lah lah.

Then mummy and daddy came over to me and they said we were going home. But that everything was really all right. Mummys eye was all purple. She looked funny, like a lady on the television.

Daisy said owie, I told her yes, it was an owie. We got back in the car.

On the way home, nobody said anything. The baby sleeped.

There was a dead animal by the side of the road somebody had hit with a car. Daddy said it was a white deer. I thought it was the unicorn, but mummy told me that you cant kill unicorns but I think she was lying like grownups do again.

When we got to Twilight I said, if you told someone your wish, did that mean it wouldnt come true?

What wish, said Daddy?

Your birthday wish. When you blow out the candles.

He said, Wishes dont come true whether you tell them or not. Wishes, he said. He said you cant trust wishes.

I asked Mummy, and she said, whatever your father says, she said in her cold voice, which is the one she uses when she tells me off with my whole name.

Then I sleeped too.

And then we were home, and it was morning, and I dont want to see the end of the world again. And before I got out of the car, while mummy was carrying in Daisydaisy to the house, I closed my eyes so I couldn't see anything at all, and I wished and I wished and I wished and I wished. I wished wed gone to Ponydale. I wished wed never gone anywhere at all. I wished I was somebody else.

And I wished.

*   *   *

NEIL GAIMAN is the author of the cult graphic novel series, *The Sandman* (1989–96) which, in its 2,000 pages, combines the subjects of myth, folklore, magic and New Age interests in a type of storytelling that has proved the forerunner to the Harry Potter and *Buffy the Vampire Slayer* phenomena. One episode of the series won the World Fantasy Award in 1991 and apart from millions of admirers around the world, *Sandman* has been praised by Stephen King and Tori Amos among many others. Neil Gaiman has also demonstrated an amazingly versatile imagination in other graphic series like *Black Orchid* (1988–9); in a collaboration with Terry Pratchett, *Good Omens – The Nice and Accurate Prophecies of Agnes Nutter, Witch* (1990); a BBC TV series, *Neverwhere* (1996); and, most recently, a best-selling novel, *American Gods* (2001) about an America teeming with ancient gods who have been brought to the country by immigrants and then forgotten all about.

Although he was born in England, Neil Gaiman now lives in Minnesota in a big house where, he says, 'I grow exotic pumpkins and accumulate computers and cats.' He worked initially in London as a journalist, interviewer and reviewer before becoming a freelance writer. The success of the *Sandman* series freed him to produce other graphic stories and fiction as well as writing scripts for television and films. All of which, he says, is a kind of tribute to the scary books he used to sit reading when he was a youngster just as you, the reader, have now done. Here's to the next scare!

ACKNOWLEDGEMENTS

The editor and publishers are grateful to the following authors, their publishers and agents for permission to include copyright stories in this collection:

'Video Nasty' by Philip Pullman. Reprinted by permission of Philip Pullman and his agents, A.P. Watt Ltd.
'The House of No Return' by R.L. Stine. Reprinted by permission of the author and his publishers, Scholastic Inc.
'Finders Keepers' by Anne McCaffrey. Reprinted by permission of MBA Literary Agents Ltd.
'The Black Dress' by Alison Prince. Reprinted by permission of the Jennifer Luithlen Agency.
'Cloud Cover' by Robert Swindells. Reprinted by permission of the Jennifer Luithlen Agency.
'The Ghost Horse of Genghis Khan' by Russell Hoban. Reprinted by permission of the author and his agents, David Higham Associates.
'Kittens' by Dean Koontz. Copyright © 1966 by Dean R. Koontz; revised version in 1995. Reprinted by permission of the author.
'Horror Snap' by Pete Johnson. Reprinted by permission of the Jennifer Luithlen Agency.
'When We Went To See The End Of The World by Dawnie Morningside, Age $11\frac{1}{4}$' by Neil Gaiman. Reprinted by permission of Headline Book Publishing Ltd.